THE WITCHES OF KYIV
AND OTHER GOTHIC TALES

SELECTED WORKS OF OREST SOMOV

Translation: Svitlana Yakovenko
Editor: Catherine Etteridge
Cover design: Colin Thompson
Designer: Volodymyr Zavgorodny

ISBN: 978-0-9945334-0-1 (Paperback)
ISBN: 978-0-9945334-1-8 (PDF)
ISBN: 978-0-9875943-9-6 (EPUB)

SOVA
BOOKS

Acknowledgement

Our sincere gratitude goes to the wonderful staff of the National Art Museum of Ukraine, especially Lesia Tolstova and Yuliya Lytvynets, who advised on, selected and supplied copies of the Ukrainian artworks that accompany Orest Somov's stories in this edition.

CONTENTS

FOREWORD

THE UNKNOWN UKRAINIAN:
OREST SOMOV'S PROSE AS A WINDOW
TO EARLY NINETEENTH-CENTURY UKRAINE

Orest Somov (1793–1833), a Ukrainian Romantic author, literary critic, translator and essayist of the pre-Shevchenko period, has been unduly forgotten by the reading public in Ukraine and might not be well known to the English reader. Reasons for his obscurity vary, but the two most obvious ones are his contested position between the Ukrainian and Russian national canons and his short-lived literary fame, quickly overshone by his younger contemporary, Nikolai Gogol / Mykola Hohol (1809–1852). Even when rescued from oblivion by post-Soviet literary critics, Somov is still called a Russian author and delegated to the realm of the Russian canon, despite his Ukrainian origins and the prominence of Ukrainian themes in his tales – a tradition, reflective of Ukraine's presumed cultural subservience to Russia, cultivated by the Imperial and, later, Soviet regimes.[i]

Recently, Iurii Vynnychuk put Somov back on the Ukrainian literary radar by including his works in popular editions of the Ukrainian Gothic.[ii] With its collection of Somov's folktales, Sova

---

[i]   See Marina Zhurina's recent dissertation *Tvorcheskaia evoliutsiia O. M. Somova i problemy folklorizma* [O. M. Somov's Creative Evolution and the Issue of Folklorism] (Cheboksary: Iakovlev Chuvash State Pedagogical University, 2007) that presents Somov as 'deiatel russkoi kultury i literatury XIX veka' [nineteenth-century Russian writer and cultural activist]: http://www.dissercat.com/content/tvorcheskaya-evolyutsiya-om-somova-i-problemy-folklorizma 4 June 2016.

[ii] Iurii Vynnychuk, compl. *Ohnianyi Zmii: Ukrainska hotychna proza XIX st.* [The Fire-Breathing Dragon: Ukrainian Gothic Prose of the 19th Century]

Books adds to the revival of Somov's legacy and breaks the Soviet discourse that viewed Somov, alongside Gogol and other Ukrainians who wrote in Russian, as a Russian author. Not only does the editor and the translator, Svitlana Yakovenko, reclaim Somov for Ukraine's literary canon, but her English translation helps to break the void surrounding Ukraine in the global cultural arena[iii] by giving its authors the international exposure they deserve.

So, who was Somov, and why is his legacy still contested by Russia and Ukraine? Descendant of an impoverished Ukrainian landed gentry, Somov was a graduate of Kharkiv University, one of the major centres of cultural and intellectual thought in the Russian Empire and a scholarly cradle that gave birth to the nineteenth-century Ukrainian national awakening. When the twenty-something Somov – young, ambitious and educated – arrived in St Petersburg, the metropolitan capital of the Russian Empire, to make a name for himself, he found there a cultural *milieu* not unlike the one he experienced at home. St Petersburg introduced him to a group of Ukrainian expatriates who formed a cultural island representing his homeland and whose ranks he joined ardently.[iv] On the wings of the Romantic philosophy that turned away from imitating the classics and called for something new, unique, and fresh, he advocated for the formation of a literary canon, based on the voice of the people (*narod*), previously ignored by the intellectuals. In his famous essay *On Romantic Poetry* (1823), Somov turns attention to the native mythology, songs, poetry and history of the peoples of the Russian Empire. Like Walter Scott, who incorporated the lore of his native Scotland into his historical novels, Somov based his unfinished novel *Haidamaka* on Ukrainian history and folklore (1827), weaving

---

(Lviv: Literaturna ahentsiia 'Piramida', 2006). Vynnychuk's edition includes three tales 'Rusalka', 'The Witches of Kyiv', and 'The Evil Eye' (that are also part of the present collection), as well as an excerpt from his novella *Tales of Buried Treasure,* all in Ukrainian translation.

[iii] Many contemporary Ukrainian authors, cultural and civic activists spoke on this problem. For a more recent statement, see Oksana Zabuzhko's article 'One Hundred Years of Solitude, or The Importance of a Story', *AGNI Online* April 2016: http://www.bu.edu/agni/essays/online/2016/zabuzhko.html 3 May 2016.

[iv] John Mersereau, Jr. in his *Orest Somov: Russian Fiction Between Romanticism and Realism* (Ann Arbor: Ardis, 1989, p. 14) states that, among others, Somov met the following countrymen in St Petersburg: Prince Nikolai Tsertelev / Mykola Tserteliev and Vasilii Tumanskii / Vasyl Tumanskyi. Furthermore, Somov regularly corresponded with another Ukrainian, Mikhail Maksimovich / Mykhailo Maksymovych, who worked and lived in Moscow (pp. 26-36).

the 'Robin Hood' style tale into events of the Ukrainian peasant uprisings against the Polish nobility in the late eighteenth century (known as the *haidamak* movement). This novel became the first in a series of literary works on Ukrainian themes that he published between then and 1833, the year of his untimely death.

Well-travelled and part of the imperial intelligentsia, Somov also published works on topics other than Ukraine, incorporating Russian folklore and trying his hand in the genres of travel writing and society tales by depicting the provincial *milieu* of the Russian empire and a broad social range of characters.[v] Somov wrote in Russian, the *lingua franca* of the Russian Empire, and his emphasis on the prose forms and everyday language led to the growth of Russian as a literary language.[vi] It was these efforts that led to his absorption by the Russian literary canon, but his contribution to the Ukrainian literary scene was no less. His Ukrainian tales made a big impact on the literary canon of the 1820s and became the subject of a literary dialogue.[vii] To give just one example, Aleksandr Pushkin, the preeminent Russian Romantic and founder of modern Russian literature, revisited Somov's 'The Witches of Kyiv', the inaugural tale in this collection and one of his most famous works, in his own writing.[viii] It is thanks to Somov's efforts that, a few years later, young Gogol asked his mother in his letter home, dated 30 April 1829, to send him as much ethnographical material as possible, seeing that everyone in the imperial capital was captivated by all things Ukrainian.[ix] Gogol himself used Somov's writing as inspiration. In particular, the same tale, 'The Witches of Kyiv', is seen by some scholars as a predecessor to Gogol's heavily mythologised and

---

[v]   Discussed by Mersereau in *Orest Somov* pp. 130, 154.

[vi] See Mersereau, *Orest Somov* pp. 45-46, 153. See also N. N. Petrunina, 'Orest Somov i ego proza' [Orest Somov and His Prose] in O. M. Somov, *Byli i nebylitsy* [Legends and Tales] (Moscow: 'Sovetskaia Rossiia', 1984) p. 14.

[vii] Z. V. Kyryliuk, *O. Somov – Krytyk ta beletryst pushkinskoi epokhy* [O. Somov – Literary Critic and Belletrist of the Pushkin Epoch] (Kyiv: Vydavnytstvo Kyivskoho universytetu, 1965).

[viii] See Zhurina's recent dissertation *Tvorcheskaia evoliutsiia O. M. Somova i problemy folklorizma*; Mersereau's *Orest Somov* p. 82; Kyryliuk, *O. Somov* p. 130.

[ix] Kyryliuk, *O. Somov* p. 111.

intensely psychological *Vii*.[x] Somov's success as a portraitist of Ukrainian life is summed up by John Mersereau, Jr., who states:

> Although Somov did a creditable job of characterization in those of his stories with foreign settings, such as the insouciant barber Achilles in 'The Springboard', he was more consistently successful in describing Slavs, in particular Ukrainians. Just as he sought to preserve as many as possible of the rapidly disappearing Ukrainian folk legends, he also strove to embody in his works types characteristic of his native region.[xi]

Writing under the pseudonym of Porfirii Baiskii, Somov brings up two topics that will become of interest to subsequent generations of Ukrainian authors in their construction of Ukrainian literary and national discourse: Ukraine's Cossacks (Kozaks), especially the Bohdan Khmelnytskyi period that served as a foundation for the Ukrainian national movement of the nineteenth century, and the earlier time of the Kyivan Rus. His choice of themes is influenced by the general interest in the national history of the time, seen in the anonymously published monograph *Istoriia Rusiv* [History of Rus], and by the richness of Ukrainian folklore related to those periods, including old beliefs, remnants of pre-Christian Rus, and the historical songs, *dumy,* from the Cossack period. But history and folklore are not the only focal points of his writing. Ukrainian people and their spirit is the major theme in the writings of this early advocate of Romanticism.[xii]

---

[x]   Among other sources, Zhurina points to B. Ia. Vilenchik's article 'Vozmozhnye istochniki stikhotvoreniia Pushkina 'Gusar'' [On Plausible Sources of Pushkin's Poem 'The Hussar'] that links Gogol's *Vii* to Somov: http://www.dissercat. com/content/tvorcheskaya-evolyutsiya-om-somova-i-problemy-folklorizma 4 June 2016.

[xi]   Mersereau, *Orest Somov* p. 58.

[xii]   All of the above-mentioned critics speak of Somov's literary engagement with Ukraine. Mersereau brings up an interesting fact that, based on the predominance of Ukrainian themes in his writing, several critics referred to Somov as a Ukrainian author, but he does not cite any names (p. 53). He later adds a statement that such national delineation does Somov an injustice, limiting the impact of his creative contribution. Writing in the 1980s, Mersereau must still have had in mind Ukraine's subordinate status within the Russian Empire and later Soviet Union. Hence, his comment about the

The present collection comprises six tales that draw on Ukrainian folklore, which Somov published between 1827 and 1833. One of his most known works and the titular tale in this edition, 'The Witches of Kyiv', already saw the light of day in English within a collection of translated fantastic prose under a telling title: *Russian 19th-century Gothic Tales* (Moscow: Raduga, 1984).[xiii] The other five – 'Rusalka', 'The Evil Eye', 'Wandering Light', 'Kupalo Eve', and 'God's Fool' – are coming out in English translation for the first time.[xiv] In addition to the common theme of Ukraine (Ukrainian setting, customs, history, beliefs and people) that unites these works, all of them also draw on the Gothic literary tradition. Somov knew it very well, as seen from a tale (a prose version of Robert Southey's ballad *Mary, the Maid of the Inn*) that he wrote in imitation of the English Gothic, *Meri, ili sluzhanka traktira (Khronika odnogo mestechka v severnoi Anglii)* [Mary, or the Tavern Servant (The Chronicle of a Certain Hamlet in Northern England)] (1830), as well as from his translations of

---

limitations of the term 'Ukrainian' may stem from the fact that Mersereau understood the word 'Russian' in the phrase 'Russian literature' as 'Imperial' (or statist) rather than narrowly 'Great Russian'. Russians (i.e., Great Russians, to use the nineteenth-century terminology), like Ukrainians, were only starting to develop a 'national' literature in the empire at the beginning of the nineteenth century. Somov, like other Ukrainian authors who worked in the capital, had an empire-wide impact, contributing to the development of both Russian and Ukrainian literatures. Thus, it would be more appropriate to call Somov a Ukrainian imperial writer, rather than a 'Russian author'. Another scholar, Kyryliuk, emphasised the Ukrainian content of Somov's works in her foreword to the 1991 Ukrainian edition of his tales, but still refers to Somov as a Russian author (*russkii pisatel*); he is in fact a 'Russian-language' writer – an important distinction. With scholars challenging the Russocentric view of cultural processes in the empire (e.g., see Oleh S. Ilnytzkyj's work on Gogol's national identity and the imperial culture of the early nineteenth century), it may also be time to decolonise the interpretative lens by which Somov's writings are seen.

[xiii] Valentin Korovin, compl., *Russian 19th-century Gothic Tales* (Moscow: Raduga, 1984). Raduga edition features three tales by Somov in English translation: the above-mentioned 'The Witches of Kyiv' and his novella *Tales of Buried Treasures,* which depict a Ukrainian setting / theme, and his tale 'Werewolf', based on Russian folklore. It also includes the works of another Ukrainian, Gogol, whom it presents as Russian.

[xiv] Excerpts from four of these tales, 'Kupalo Eve', 'The Witches of Kyiv', 'The Evil Eye', and 'God's Fool', also appeared in English as quotations in Mersereau, *Orest Somov* pp. 79-80, 82-86; 126-131. His proposed translations for the titles differ slightly from the present edition.

other works of this literary movement that appeared on the pages of *Literaturnaia Gazeta* [Literary Gazette].[xv]

Based on these facts, scholars discussed possible connections between Somov and West European and American practitioners of the Gothic genre, especially the American author, Washington Irving (1783–1859), observing a specific comic nature of their Gothic prose.[xvi] Indeed, moving out of the tradition of Classicism, Somov often scorned overly metaphysical content, taking an ironic, enlightened stance towards the fantastic. However, this is not the case for all of his *oeuvre,* and definitely not for the six tales presented here. Despite occasional moments of irony, Somov, overall, takes on a very sombre tone in these tales, writing in a full-blown tradition of Romanticism. In his literary criticism, Somov spoke against blind imitation of the foreign, especially German Romantic, tradition ('German Mysticism' as he called it). Following the Decembrist poets' aesthetics to whose circle he belonged, he urged his compatriots to discover their own national cultural treasures.[xvii] It is for these reasons that he turned to his native Ukrainian folklore, drawing on the Ukrainian national character and national locale. As a result, in these tales, he blended the Western Gothic foundations with Ukrainian themes and constructed the specifically Ukrainian, indigenous world of literary horrors, thereby inaugurating the Ukrainian Gothic movement.

While being united through the use of folklore and Gothic conventions, the tales differ in their reference to historical period and, based on this, can be roughly broken into three groups. The first depicts the golden age of the Ukrainian Cossackdom of the seventeenth century ('The Witches of Kyiv', 'Rusalka' and 'The Evil Eye'); the second group references the Kyivan Rus period ('Wandering Light', 'Kupalo Eve'), and the third shows Somov's contemporary time ('God's Fool').

[xv] On Somov and the Gothic, see Mersereau, *Orest Somov* pp. 133-134, 147-148.

[xvi] See Mark S. Simpson, *The Russian Gothic Novel and Its British Antecedents* (Columbus, Ohio: Slavica Publishers, Inc., 1986) p. 95; and Vadim Vatsuro, 'Travestiia gotiki. O. Somov. A. Bestuzhev-Marlinskii,' [The Gothic Travesty. O. Somov. A. Bestuzhev-Marlinskii] in *Goticheskii roman v Rossii* [Gothic Novel in Russia] (Moscow: Novoe literaturnoe obozrenie, 2002) pp. 372-392. Needless to say, both Simpson and Vatsuro consider Somov a Russian author. See fn. xii.

[xvii] See Kyryliuk, *O. Somov* p. 104. Also, see Korovin, 'Orest Somov' (1793–1833) in *Russian 19th-century Gothic Tales* pp. 38-39.

The first group makes references to the Cossacks' glory (for example, Taras Triasylo, Cossack Hetman, and his successful campaigns of 1630 are mentioned in 'The Witches of Kyiv'), demonises the Poles, and, in the case of 'The Evil Eye', features a very poetic language, reminiscent of a Cossack *duma*. 'The Witches of Kyiv' tells a story of a dashing young Cossack Fedir Blyskavka, who comes home to settle down after his military service at the Sich, but the woman he chooses to marry, Katrusia, turns out to be an unwilling witch, made so by her mother. The story features a very gloomy ending with Katrusia killing Fedir and later suffering a violent death herself, being burned at the stake by other witches for betraying their 'guild'. While some scholars see in Fedir's death a latent punishment for involving himself in pagan rituals and forgetting about his Orthodox faith,[xviii] another interpretation of the tragic ending may be linked to the Cossack ethos that saw a move from the military to a settled or farm life as a form of metaphorical death. 'Rusalka' continues the theme of death and betrayal, but here we see both a religious and a national betrayal where a young Ukrainian girl falls in love with the enemy of the Ukrainian nation, a Pole. Such action leads her, and later her mother, to magic, forcing both to forsake their Orthodox faith. The third tale in the Cossack cluster, 'The Evil Eye', resembles a *duma* song by its language as well as its structure, appearing in the form of fourteen stanzas. Its sombre plot, featuring the untimely death of three beautiful daughters of the Cossack Mykyta, may be metaphorically interpreted as a waning time of Cossackdom, with Cossacks becoming settled and losing their military vigour, which, in turn, makes them vulnerable to hostile invasions.

The Kyivan Rus sequence consists of two tales, based on ancient Slavic beliefs and customs, that Somov wanted to preserve for posterity. The tales feature pre-Christian names of their characters (Velesyl, Mylava, Konchyslav and Nasoloda) and mention pagan Slavic Gods (Perun, Kupalo and Veles). In comparison to the previous tales, where the focus was more on women as victims of cruel fate or demonic forces (with the exception of 'The Witches

---

[xviii] M. P. Grebneva, 'O roli iazycheskikh i khristianskikh predstavlenii v povesti O. M. Somova 'Kievskie vedmy'' [On the Role of Pagan and Christian Beliefs in O. M. Somov's Long Tale 'The Witches of Kyiv']: http://cyberleninka.ru/article/n/o-roli-yazycheskih-i-hristianskih-predstavleniy-v-povesti-o-m-somova-kievskie-vedmy.pdf 5 June 2016.

of Kyiv', where Fedir occupies the reversed position of a damsel in distress), here the victims are mainly men. They are punished for their pride and anti-Christian sentiments (as in the case of Konchyslav, whose very name suggests the end of the ancient Pagan glory[xix]) or for straying off a Christian path. These tales can be linked to the preceding cycle through the image of a water-sprite (*rusalka*). However, here *rusalka* is an evil spirit that leads a Kyivan knight astray, as opposed to an innocent victim, as she is portrayed in the eponymous tale of the previous cycle, which was written later and featured a more psychologised narrative.

Finally, the last tale, 'God's Fool', introduces the supernatural to the everyday life of Somov's contemporary society. Mersereau spoke on the importance of this story in Somov's growth as an author, since it pays close attention to the psychological maturation of the main character, young officer Melskyi. This is spurred by his acquaintance with the holy fool, Vasyl, who sacrifices his life to save Melskyi.[xx] The tale draws very close to Tzvetan Todorov's concept of the fantastic, as it never offers any explanation for Vasyl's ability to see into the future and predict fate. In Mersereau's words, "The reader never knows whether [Melskyi] is facing coincidence or occult powers, and the story gains interest from this cleverly exploited tension between belief and disbelief."[xxi] Despite being placed last, this tale is the earliest among the six works selected for this edition. Its importance also lies in the fact that it shows Somov's interest not only in Ukraine's past, but also in its present.

In conclusion, the collected tales expose Somov from three angles: Somov as a Ukrainian author of the early nineteenth century, who worked in the capital of the Russian Empire but, nonetheless, thematically (as well as publicly, in his letters) showed his national allegiance to his homeland; Somov as an ethnographer, who was rushing to collect as much Ukrainian folk material as possible to preserve it for posterity;[xxii] and Somov as an initiator of an

---

[xix] Mersereau, *Orest Somov* p. 80.

[xx] Mersereau, *Orest Somov* pp. 126-131.

[xxi] Mersereau, *Orest Somov* pp. 130.

[xxii] See Somov's own footnote to that regard in his novella *Tales of Buried Treasures*. 'Читатели, конечно, поняли цель сей повести собрать сколько можно более народных преданий и поверий, распространенных в Малороссии и Украйне между простым народом, дабы оные не вовсе были потеряны для будущих археологов и поэтов.' ['Readers must have

indigenous literary tradition of the Gothic in the Ukrainian literary canon. When we look at the critical works on Somov that have appeared thus far, they are full of reference to Ukraine (for example, Zinaida Kyryliuk's 1965 monograph features a section dedicated to the Ukrainian themes in Somov's works, which is four times as long as the section on the Russian folklore/theme). However, their authors keep recycling old imperial and Soviet slogans, presenting Somov as a Russian author. I hope that the current English edition of Somov's tales, which presents him as a Ukrainian author to the world audience, will serve as the first in a series of works aimed to decolonise and reclaim this early Romantic for the Ukrainian literary canon, putting an end to the tradition of including Ukrainian authors under the collective editions of Russian prose.

Svitlana Krys, PhD
MacEwan University
Edmonton, AB Canada

---

guessed that the goal of this novella is to collect as many of the folktales and beliefs that are popular among the simple folk in Little Russia and Ukraine as possible, so that they will not be lost to future archeologists and poets.']
Somov, 'Skazki o kladakh' [Tales of Buried Treasure], in *Byli i nebylitsy* p. 217, fn. vii.

THE WITCHES OF KYIV

1833

A young kozak from a Kyivan regiment, Fedir Blyskavka, had returned to his homeland from a campaign to liberate Ukraine[1] from her oppressors, the Poles. Taras Triasylo, a brave Hetman of the Ukrainian army had driven the Poles from many Ukrainian towns since the famous Taras Night, when he defeated the arrogant Koniecpolski. [...] The kozaks had returned to their homes, burdened with rich spoils that they considered to be theirs by right. [...]

Those who knew Fedir Blyskavka as a dashing kozak surmised that he did not return home empty-handed. Indeed, every time he pulled a handful of ducats out of his pocket to pay a tavern-keeper or *bandura-player*[2], the Polish zlotys very nearly cascaded into the streets. At the sight of his gold the eyes of tavern-keepers and shop-keepers sparkled, and at the sight of the kozak the cheeks of maidens and young wives blushed. And with a good reason – no wonder they all called Fedir Blyskavka a dashing kozak. His tall stature and courageous bearing, his handsome and

masculine physique, his black moustache, which he twirled proudly, his youth, good looks and courage could sweep any woman off her feet. Is it any wonder that young Kyivan women looked at him with playful and welcoming smiles, and that each of them was overjoyed when he spoke to them or allowed himself some harmless liberty in his conduct towards them?

The street hawkers of Pechersk and Podil[3], all of them, from the first to the last, knew him. With contentment on their faces they winked to each other when he walked through the market. They waited for these visits like a raven waits for blood because Fedir Blyskavka, with his kozak swagger, would bump their trays laden with *knyshy*[4], *slastiony*[5] or cherries and send large mounds of watermelons and rockmelons rolling in all directions, but would then compensate them for everything at three times the usual price.

"Why haven't we seen our mischievous lad for so long?" remarked one of the Podil hawkers to her neighbour. "Without him, trade is so very different – you can sit all day without making a tenth of what you could make from him in one moment."

"He has no time for all that now!" her neighbour answered. "You see, he is fawning after Katrusia Lantsiuhivna. Since he met her, he stopped showing himself at the markets."

"And why wouldn't Lantsiuhivna be a good match for him?" the third street hawker thrust herself into the conversation. "That young lady is as beautiful as a poppy flower; one look at her and you can't help saying: 'She is a beauty!' Her hair is raven, her eyebrows and eyes are jet-black, her figure is flawless; a single smile from her drives all the lads insane. And her mother is not a poor woman either – although she is stingy, the old hag – in fact, she has money to burn."

"All this is true," the first street hawker butted in, "but only ill repute follows the old Lantsiuzhykha. Everyone says – Lord have mercy on us – that she is a witch."

"I also heard those stories, dear," the second hawker remarked. "Once my neighbour Panchokha saw with his own eyes how the old Lantsiuzhykha flew out of the chimney and travelled, apparently, to the Sabbath..."

"There are plenty of tales one can tell about her!" – the first hawker interrupted her. "She drove Petro Dziubenko's cow to death and poisoned the Yurchevskys' dogs, as one of them was a *yarchuk*[6] and could sniff out a witch. Because of the quarrel about

Detail of: *At the Fairground* by Serhiy Svitoslavskyi.

the vegetable garden with Nychypor Protaliy she did such things to him that I can hardly dare mention."

"What? What was it?" the other two cried with curiosity.

"Well, whatever will be, will be, I have to tell you. The old Lantsiuzhykha turned Nychypor's daughter into a good-for-nothing. Now, poor Dokyika meows and scratches the walls like a cat, or barks and bares her teeth like a dog, or squawks and hops on one leg like a magpie..."

"Enough of this idle talk, you chatterboxes!" their conversation was interrupted by an old street hawker with an evil appearance, who fixed them with the stare of a vicious dog when it growls at passers-by. "You would be better off talking about yourselves rather than others," she snarled abruptly and angrily. "You believe all elderly women with money to be witches, but you do not look back to check your own tails."

Involuntarily, all the street hawkers cried out at the old woman's last words, but they calmed down instantly because they did not dare to quarrel with her. A quiet rumour about her had been circulating, a rumour that she also belonged to the coven of Kyivan witches.

Although there were good people who tried to warn Fedir Blyskavka against marrying Katrusia Lantsiuhivna, the young kozak laughed in their faces and had no intention of leaving Katrusia. How could he believe those rumours? The darling girl looked at him so innocently and so kind-heartedly, and she smiled at him so sweetly that, even if the whole of Kyiv had gathered in the town square and sworn that her mother was in fact a witch, even then, Fedir would not believe it.

He brought back his young wife to be the mistress of his home. The old Lantsiuzhykha remained in her house, and refused the invitation of her son-in-law to move in with them, explaining her decision that she, in her old habits, would not be able to get along with young people.

There was no limit to Fedir Blyskavka's happiness and pride when he looked at his dear wife. Her passionate caresses and fervent kisses, her pandering to her husband's needs and her mastery of household matters – everything pleased our kozak. The only strange thing he found with her was that sometimes, in the middle of the sweetest expressions of conjugal tenderness, she suddenly became sad, sighed heavily, and even tears appeared in her eyes; and sometimes he noticed such a gaze in her big black eyes that it sent a shiver down his spine. In particular he noticed that gaze around the end of each month. Then his wife became gloomy, answered him curtly and reluctantly, and it seemed that some kind of longing gnawed at her heart. At those times everything bothered her: her husband's affection, his friends' greetings or household chores; it was as if this world of God was smothering her, as if she was being drawn somewhere but with repulsion and under extreme coercion, as if responding to some irresistible enticement. At times it was noticeable that she wanted to open up to her husband about something, but every time the burdensome secret remained lying heavily in her bosom and oppressing her. Only a deathly pallor, a flood of tears and the trembling of her whole body betrayed to her husband that something had gone awry; he could gain no other confession from her.

Then, at once mastering herself, Katrusia would brighten up, begin to laugh, have fun like a child and show more affection towards her husband than ever. She would convince him that it was an attack caused by a curse put on her when she was still a little girl, by the evil eye of some vicious old woman, but that it never lasted for long. Fedir believed his wife because he loved her and, moreover, because he had seen examples of such curses or afflictions.

However, at nightfall as the moon was waning, he always noticed his wife's strange restlessness. It seemed that she was beginning to fear something, every instant quivering and turning paler by the hour. He wanted to learn the cause of it, but that was beyond his powers – each time when, in the evening, he noticed in Katrusia some anxiety, some worries, a strange, deep sleep would overcome him as soon as he put his head on his pillow.

Whether he hit upon the idea himself or whether good people gave him the advice, Fedir, on a night when the moon was waning, climbed into bed and searched with his hand beneath his pillow until he found a bundle of herbs. As soon as he touched it, he suddenly felt his hand begin to grow heavy and the blood slowing in it, little by little, as if falling asleep. His wife at that moment was preoccupied with her household chores and did not watch him. Fedir instantly opened a top windowpane and threw out the herb bundle. Their watchdog, which lay upon the *pryzba*[7], probably thought it had been thrown a bone or some other treat; it stood up, shook itself, and in one jump landed near the bundle and began sniffing it, but at the first sniff the dog staggered and fell, immersed in a deep slumber.

Detail of: *At the River* by Mykola Pymonenko.

"Aha! So this is what made me sleep, my dear wifey!" thought Fedir. His doubts were partially confirmed, but, in order to completely prove the dreadful secret and avoid his wife's suspicion, he pretended to be asleep and started snoring as though he had been deprived of sleep for three days.

Katrusia, having returned from the larder where she had taken the remains of their dinner, approached her husband, put her hand on his chest, looked him in his face and then, with a heavy sigh, went to the stove. Maintaining a snore for all he was worth, Fedir Blyskavka half-opened his eyes and observed his wife. He saw how she started the fire in the stove, placed a pot with water on the coals and began to throw in some herbs, chanting strange words in a low voice that he was unaccustomed to hearing. Fedir's agitation was increasing with every minute: fear, rage and curiosity fought within him; finally, the latter prevailed. Pretending to be asleep, he watched what was going to happen next.

When the water in the pot started boiling, it was as if a storm raged, a heavy rain pounded, and a strong thunder boomed over it; then finally, in a squeaky and sharp voice like the rasp of iron, three words sounded: "Fly, fly, fly!" At this moment, Katrusia quickly rubbed some ointment on herself, then flew up through the chimney.

The poor kozak was so overcome with trembling that he could not keep his teeth from chattering. Now no doubts remained: his wife was a witch; he had seen with his own eyes how she was making herself ready and then flying off to the Sabbath. What should he do? Overcome with a tumult of feelings and anguish of the heart he could think of nothing to do. He did not even have enough courage to act – he decided it would be better to defer it until the next occasion to allow more time to think everything over, to prepare for anything and to summon up some courage. However, sleeplessness continued to torture him and fear chased his dreams away; hideous monsters kept appearing before his eyes. He tossed and turned in his bed, then rose and walked around the house, but all in vain! Sleep eluded him and he was stifled in the house. He went outside into the fresh air where the quiet and cool night refreshed him a little. The moon, with its last pale light, seemed to bid farewell to the earth until its next resurrection. Under its feeble shimmering light Fedir saw the sleeping dog and the spellbound bundle beside it. In order to banish the wearying sleeplessness and to hide from his wife that he had learnt her secret, Fedir picked up the bundle of herbs with two splinters; at once, the dog stirred, jumped up, shook its head and started to nuzzle its master. Without wasting any time, the young kozak returned to the house, placed the bundle under his pillow, lay down on it and slept like a log.

When he opened his eyes, he saw Katrusia lying next to him. There was no trace of yesterday's insanity on her face, nor the frantic savagery, with which she had chanted incantations, in her eyes. Some languid bliss, some quiet joy reflected in her eyes and in her smile. Never before had she bestowed so many impassioned kisses upon and shared so much affection with her husband as that morning. In short, she was a young, sweet and loving woman, an uncomplicated and playful creature, certainly not the terrible sorceress her husband had seen the previous night. It seemed that it was not and there could not be pretence in her: she lived only for their love and saw all the happiness of life only in her beloved husband. The kozak began to doubt himself: indeed, did it really happen, all that he had witnessed? Could he have dreamt all that last night? Was it some evil spirit that troubled him with horrible nightmares, in order to alienate his heart from his dear wife?

Another month passed. During all that time, Katrusia was a hardworking, gentle and cheerful young woman, an affectionate and caring wife. Yet secretly Fedir Blyskavka pondered on what he should do, and finally he came to a decision. By the waning of the moon he began to watch his wife intently and he noticed the same signs as before: tears, heavy sighs, hidden yearning, revulsion towards everything – even to her husband's affections – and, on occasions, a feral, fixed gaze.

Early in the evening Fedir announced that it was stuffy in the house, and opened the window; however, when he was getting into bed, he put his hand under the pillow, grabbed the herb bundle and threw it into the yard with the swiftness he would normally use to cast off a burning coal he had taken from the stove to light his pipe. It was done in no time, so that Katrusia could not notice anything. Rejoicing with success, the kozak pretended to be asleep and snored away, as he did on the first occasion.

As she did previously, his wife came up to the bed and looked at his face, put her hand on his chest, leaned over and kissed her husband, and he felt a hot tear fall on his cheek. Then, with a heavy sigh and wiping off her eyes with a sleeve of her delicate blouse, she commenced her heretic task. This time the kozak, supported by his firm determination and courage, redoubled his attention. He watched what herbs his wife was taking, and from where, and he listened to the strange words and memorised them. Nothing scared him any longer: neither his wife's frantic fierce face, nor her flaming eyes, nor the roar of the storm, nor thunder, nor the shrill and hideous voice from the pot.

As soon as the young witch disappeared into the chimney, her husband jumped out of bed, threw more firewood into the dying embers, poured fresh water into a pot and placed it on the fire. Then he found a small chest, hidden beneath a bench under the floorboards and covered by stones – opening it, he froze in horror and disgust. There were human bones and hair, dried bats and toads, snakeskin, wolf's teeth, belemnites[8], aspen charcoal, black cat bones, a great variety of strange shells, dried herbs and roots and... more than one could remember. Having overcome his disgust, Fedir grabbed a handful of the magic supplies and threw them into the cauldron, chanting the words that he had heard from his wife. But when the cauldron began to boil, Fedir felt his face grimacing and twitching as if from convulsions; his eyeballs strayed, his hair stood on end, in his chest it felt as if someone was hammering, and all his bones tremored in their joints. After that he went into a kind of trance and felt an exorbitant courage, something resembling an extreme degree of intoxication: bright sparks, light stripes and some strange ugly apparitions alternately flashed before his eyes; over him a storm raged, rain drummed down and thunder roared, but now he did not fear anything. When he heard a loud and harsh voice from the pot saying: "Fly, fly, fly!" – in a state of madness that came over him, making him lose self-control, he hastily grabbed a box of ointment, rubbed it on his arms, legs, face and chest... and at once some invisible force grabbed his body and threw him into the chimney. This rapid movement deprived him of his breath and his memory. When he gained consciousness, he found himself under the open sky on the hill of *Lysa Hora*[9], outside Kyiv...

What our brave kozak witnessed there, probably no other orthodox Christian had ever seen; and God forbid they ever do! Both fear and laughter seized him alternately – so horrible and so ugly was the gathering on Lysa Hora! Fortunately, there was a huge aspen wood bonfire not far from Fedir Blyskavka; he hid behind the bonfire and peeked through it like a mouse that, from its hole, peeps into a house full of people and cats.

At the very top of the hill was a smooth clearing, black as coal and bald as the hairless head of an old man. This gave rise to the hill's name, 'Lysa Hora'. In the middle of the clearing stood a platform that had seven steps and was covered with black cloth. On it sat a huge bear with two monkey faces, a goat's horns, a snake's tail, a hedgehog's spiny coat all over his body, skeleton arms and a cat's claws on his fingers.

Around it, at some distance from the glade, was a whole bazaar of witches, warlocks, *upyri*[10], *perevertni*[11], *lisovyky*[12], *vodianyky*[13], *domovyky*[14] and all sorts of other unseen and unheard of creatures. A giant squatted in front of a cimbalom, the size of a barge, with the strings as thick as a rope; the giant played the cimbalom with huge rakes, shaking his pointed beard, blinking his eyes and distorting his already hideous face. Nearby a whole gang of small *chorty*[15], each one more heinous and clumsier than the other, banged on cauldrons, drummed on kegs, beat iron plates and bawled at the tops of their voices. Then a string of old witches, shrivelled like mushrooms, led the *zhuravel*[16] dance, and capering beat the *hotsak*[17] with their scraggy feet so hard that the sound of their bones could be heard all around, and sang in such a voice that it hurt one's ears. A bit further on, leggy *lisovyky* hoofed it with dwarf *domovyky*. Elsewhere, toothless and decrepit witches rode their brooms, shovels and stove forks, pompously and arrogantly, like noble ladies dancing the polonaise, with gray and ugly warlocks – one who was bent into an arc from old age, another whose nose hung over his lips and clung to his chin, and yet a third with two fangs sticking out of the edges of his mouth, and the fourth with as many wrinkles on his forehead as there were waves travelling along the Dnieper in stormy weather. Young witches with frantic and manic laughter and the shrieks of drunken women at a party, danced the *horlytsia*[18] and the *metelytsia*[19] with scruffy *vodianyky*, whose ugly faces were covered with slime two-fingers-thick; the mischievous and playful *rusalky*[20] floated swiftly in a dance with *upyri*, who were too hideous to look at. Shouting, roaring, clattering, scuffles, the shrill squeaks and whistles of hellish horns and *sopilky*[21], the singing and screeching of small *chorty* and witches – all that was rambunctious, wild and savage – bore evidence that those devilish creatures enjoyed the fun without inhibitions.

From his hiding place Fedir Blyskavka saw it all, and he was so terrified that coldness gripped all his insides. Not far from his place, he noticed his mother-in-law, Lantsiuzhykha, with a beekeeper from across the Dnieper, who always had a bad reputation clinging to him; old Odarka Shvoyda, who used to sell *bublyky*[22] at the Podil market, was with a ninety-year-old shop-owner Artiukh Kholoziy, whom everyone revered almost as a saint because this wretched hypocrite could pretend so well to be pious and humble; poverty-stricken crippled Motria, who begged on the streets of Kyiv, where the good people took her for God's fool and nicknamed her Dzyha, and here she was walking hand in hand with a rich miser, Pan Krupka, a landowner who recently had been driven out by the kozaks from Kyiv and who was also hated by his countrymen, the Poles, for taking bribes. Fedir Blyskavka saw many others of his acquaintances, including even those who he would never have believed to be devil worshippers, even if his own father had sworn to it under oath.

The whole crowd of old witches and warlocks embarked on a dance so fervently that even the dust arose; they would have been the envy of the most daredevil kozaks and most brazen young women. A little further to the side, Fedir noticed his wife. Katrusia danced the *kozachok*[23] with a broad-shouldered and sharp-horned *lisovyk*, who grinned and winked at her, while she smiled back and spun around in front of him, like a spinning top. Filled with rage and jealousy, Fedir was ready to pounce on her and her horned dance partner and give them a hiding. However, on reflection he resisted his impulse and acted sensibly. How would he be able to cope with the whole coven of witches, who would probably attack him, and then it would mean certain death for him?

All of a sudden, like the unexpected windgust from a storm, the thick and hoarse roar of the Black Bear sitting on the platform blared out and subdued all: the sounds of horns and cimbalom, the whistles of bagpipes and *sopilky*, the shouts, laughter and chatter of the cheerful crowd. Everything went still: all the dancers, having lifted one foot in the air, froze as if rooted to the ground with their other foot; those who jumped up remained suspended in the air; mouths left open had no time to shut; arms elevated during the dance and raised shoulders and heads had no time to drop down. The giant's rakes on the cimbalom and the little *chorty*'s bows on the fiddles stopped dead upon the strings. The Black Bear stretched his skeleton arm forward – and instantly they all sang:

A magpie's jumps
Are high,
A crow's bows
Are low.

Everyone jumped up then fell upon the ground, with their heads towards the place where the Black Bear sat.

"Oh, you are a damned lot!" Fedir Blyskavka whispered to himself. "They even dare to blaspheme the rites of the Orthodox faith and sing decent songs at their disgusting Sabbath in front of this monster, in mockery of all good people! May you all fall into hell, and take my wifey with you; may you all get a burning firebrand down your throats: then, for sure, you would forget how to bellow and start singing a different song, Devil's horde!"

For a while the Black Bear sniffed in all directions and finally roared, as if from within a barrel: "A stranger is in our midst!"

In an instant a commotion broke out: the evil spirits, witches, warlocks, *upyri* and *rusalky* all rushed to search with their savage and bloodshot eyes while rage foamed from their mouths. And Katrusia, his Katrusia, was one of the first! Fedir's heart sank and shivers ran down his spine. "Now," the kozak thought, "comes my hour of death!" Shrinking into the ground behind the firewood he peeked out, half dead with fright. Suddenly he saw Katrusia running towards his hiding place; she looked behind the bonfire, angrily flashed her fiery eyes at her husband and gnashed her teeth... but at that very moment she tore off her kerchief, threw it over Fedir, pushed a shovel beneath him and made a line in the air with her finger towards Kyiv – and before Fedir realised what had happened, he was lying on his bed at home.

When his feelings subsided a little, he sat on the bed, like a man barely recovered from a fever that had given him terrible nightmares. Soon his thoughts began to right themselves: he recollected both the horrors, uproariousness and the disgusting tomfoolery of the previous night, and of his wife, with her love, her gentle affection and her thoughtfulness towards him and to their home and her childlike playfulness...

"And all that was only a pretence!" he thought. "The evil force whispered all that to her in order to deceive me better."

Suddenly he would experience visions of his wife, either at the moment of the witchcraft rites, or flashing her fiery look at him and gnashing her teeth as she did on Lysa Hora... Deep in thought, he did not notice that his wife stood beside him. Fedir looked at her and shuddered, as if he had stepped on a snake with his bare foot. Katrusia was ashen and drained, her lips were lifeless and her eyes red with the tears that flowed in streams down her face.

"Fedir," she asked sadly, "why were you prying into what I did? Why did you venture to Lysa Hora without asking me? Why didn't you confide in your wife? God be with you! You yourself have demolished our happiness!"

"Get away from me, snake, temptress and repellent witch!" replied Fedir with resentment and disgust. "So, you want to charm me again with your devilish flattery? This time you won't have a hope!"

"Listen, Fedir," she entreated, throwing her arms around his body, leaning her head on his chest and looking beseechingly into his eyes. "Listen! I am not to blame, it is my mother's doing: she forcibly took me to the Sabbath, forcefully doomed me to become a witch and extorted a terrible oath from me... I was only fourteen years old. Back then I flew to the Sabbath, reluctantly fearing my mother: the witches with all their accursed ceremonies and all their damned rites were like a sharp knife to me, and one thought of the Sabbath made me sick to my soul. Just imagine how it was for me when you became my husband – you, whom I love as my soul, as my salvation in the other world... Many times I wanted to abandon the Sabbath and never be part of it again, yet by the waning of the moon the more I thought about it, the more I was tormented by unspeakable anguish. You know yourself how I felt then... You would not wish that on your worst enemy! No matter how hard I fought to overcome the heavy gloom, no matter how much I prayed – all was in vain! Day and night, something was breathing into my ear about the Sabbath; I was constantly drawn towards going there. And when the day came, some invisible force dragged me there, in spite of my will. When I arrived at Lysa Hora it was like some madness came over me: I dived wildly into the crowd of witches, warlocks and all the other demonic creatures; I was not in charge of my own actions and could not but do what the others did... I was waiting for the Holy Week as if I were waiting for God to come down from Heaven so then I could throw myself at the feet of holy monks and beg them to lock me away for the last three days in the caves[24] until Easter Sunday matins, and pray to exorcise the

Detail of: *Shchekavytsia, Kniaz Oleh's Burial Site* by Mykhailo Sazhyn.

demonic obsession... Now it is too late! You, my dear husband, my beloved, you destroyed both me and yourself, and forever closed the gates of paradise to me..."

"Then go and live with your own kind, with *lisovyky* and *rusalky*, if the pathway to where the Christian souls rejoice is closed to you! Be gone from here! Leave me..."

"It is not up to me to leave you!" Katrusia interrupted him, embracing him tighter in her arms, so to speak, becoming one with him. "I told you that I gave a terrible oath... Because of this oath, if any of our loved ones – either husband, or brother, or father... no matter who he is – spies on our rituals, then we must... Oh! It is so hard to say!... We must drink their blood until the last drop..."

"Then drink my blood! I am sick of living in this world! What is my life? I fell in love with one woman and she became my wife; I love her more than a beautiful day, more than joy itself, but even she deceived me and almost made me a part of the satanic family... Everything repels me in this world... Drink, suck my blood!"

"Without you, I too will have no life in the world! Your soul will see that. It is so sad, it is so hard that an evil fate has parted us, in this world and in the other..." Katrusia started sobbing and fell at her husband's feet.

"I beg of you one thing only," she continued, "look at me affectionately and let me have a good look at you; kiss me for the last time and press me to your heart as you would do when you loved me!"

Kind Fedir was moved by his wife's tearful requests. He looked at her tenderly, embraced her and their lips united together into one long and hot kiss... At that very moment her hand sought out his heart by its beat. All of a sudden a sharp, burning spark penetrated Fedir's heart; he felt both agony and a pleasant languor. Katrusia clung to his heart and pressed her lips to it; and while Fedir was melting in a bliss of luxurious slumber, Katrusia asked him affectionately: "Is it delightful to fall asleep like this?"

"Delightful!" He answered in a barely audible murmur and fell asleep forever.

The kozak was buried with full honours by his zealous comrades. Neither his wife nor his mother-in-law were to be seen at the funeral; however, the following night the residents of Kyiv rushed to a fire – Fedir Blyskavka's house had burnt down to ashes. At the same time another glow could be seen on Lysa Hora, and the fearless lads who ventured to see it up close the following day claimed that there was no longer a huge aspen wood bonfire on the hill, but only a pile of ashes lying in its place, and stinking, sulphurous smoke wafting through the neighbourhood. The rumours circulated that the witches had burnt at the stake their young sister Katrusia because she abandoned the coven and wanted to perform Christian repentance by joining a nunnery; and that it was her mother, the old Lantsiuzhykha, who first lit the fire. Whatever happened, neither Katrusia nor Lantsiuzhykha had been seen in Kyiv since then. It was said about the latter that she turned into a wolf, and ran in the forests across the Dnieper.

Now Lysa Hora is no more than a sandy hill, overgrown with bushes on the lower slopes. It seems that the witches have abandoned it, and, as a result, it became brighter.

Rusalka

1829

Once upon a time, when our golden-domed Kyiv was under Polish rule, there lived an old woman who was the widow of a forest caretaker. Her small hut was located in the forest, where the road to the Kytaivska Pustyn[25] monastery lay. Here, with her bare hands, she eked out a living, and the only delight in her life was her sixteen-year-old daughter Horpynka. In truth, her daughter was a pure delight; she was maturing like a young cherry tree, tall and slender, and her black hair, entwined in braids, gleamed like a raven's wing beneath the coloured ribbons. Her big eyes blackened and glowed with a quiet fire like two half-extinguished coals, in which the sparks still ran. Fair-skinned, rosy-cheeked and fresh, like a young flower at dawn, she was growing up to trouble the hearts of the lads and incite the envy of the other maidens. She was the apple of her mother's eye, and God's toilers, the holy fathers of Kytaivska Pustyn, viewed her with pleasure and kindness as their future fellow in heaven whenever she came to them for a blessing.

Why did sweet Horpynka, which is how all who knew her called her, suddenly become languid and pensive? Why did she no longer sing like a bird in springtime and jump like a young billygoat? Why did she look absently at all around her and give irrelevant answers to questions? Was it a wicked wind that blew upon her, or an evil eye that stared at her, or sorcerers who had bewitched her? No! It was neither the wicked wind that blew, nor an evil eye that stared, nor sorcerers who bewitched her. In Kyiv, which back then was brimming with Poles, there was one Polish man named Casimir Chepka. Handsome in stature, fair of face, rich and from good lineage, Casimir led a carefree life: he drank Hungarian wine with friends, fought for honour using sabres and danced the krakowiak and mazurka with all the beauties. But in the summertime, being bored with the city's entertainments, he often spent the whole day wandering along the Dnieper bays and forests surrounding Kyiv shooting large and small game, whichever he came across. During one of his hunting trips he met Horpynka. The pretty girl, despite her timid and shy nature, was not afraid of his robust appearance, or his black twisted moustache, or his gun or his big gundog; she liked the young nobleman, but – even more – the young nobleman liked her. Word by word, he began to sing to her that she was beautiful, that among the city girls he did not know a single one who could compete with her in attractiveness – and who knows what else he sang to her. The first words of flattery sink deep into a young woman's heart, which somehow believes that everything said by a young handsome man must be absolutely true. Horpynka believed Casimir's words and, accidentally or deliberately, they began to meet frequently in the forest, and this was the reason why the sweet girl now became languid and pensive.

One summer evening she returned from the forest later than usual. Her mother reproached her, frightened by the prospect of wild animals and bad people. Horpynka did not answer a word; she sat down on a bench in the corner, deep in thought. She was silent for a long time, long after her mother had ceased her reprimands and sat in silence with her yarn. Suddenly, as if coming to her senses or awakening from sleep, Horpynka looked at her mother with her bright black eyes and murmured under her breath:

"Mother! I have a betrothed."

"Betrothed? Who?" the old woman asked, pausing at her spindle and looking at her daughter with concern.

During the Thunderstorm by Ivan Sokolov.

"He is not from the simple folk, mother. He is from a good family and rich: he is a young Polish nobleman..." Here, with a childlike simplicity, she told her mother everything: about the first meeting with Casimir, and her love, and his flattering promises, and her flattered hopes to be a noblewoman.

"Watch out," the old woman told her, shaking her head doubtfully, "beware of the villain; he will have his way with you, and then will leave you. Who knows what this Catholic infidel bears on his soul? And what could be worse (may God protect us!) than an evil tempter appearing to you in the Polish nobleman's image? You know that in our Kyiv, for our sins, we have many sorcerers and witches. The devil always works harder there, where people are closer to salvation."

Horpynka did not respond to this, and the conversation ended there. The sweet, innocent girl was sure that her Casimir was not a villain and not a wicked tempter, and that is why she listened to her mother's speeches with disappointment.

"He is so sweet, so kind! He will definitely keep his word, and now he is on his way to Poland in order to persuade his father and arrange his affairs. Can it be that with such a face, such a soul, such a sweet and smooth voice he could have evil designs on me? No. In her old age my mother has become too mistrustful, like all old people." With these whispers of her gullible heart the innocent young girl deluded herself. Meanwhile, the days, weeks and months passed without Casimir returning or sending any news of himself. A year passed – not a word about him had been heard. Horpynka could not find solace; the light faded from her clear eyes, and frequent sighs gripped the maiden's chest. Her mother grieved for her child's sorrow and cried sometimes, sitting alone with the yarn in her ramshackle hut. Shaking her head, she kept repeating, "No good will come! This is God's punishment for our sins and for the foolish girl falling in love with a Pole, the infidel!"

Horpynka pined away for a long time: almost incessantly she wandered the forest; she left early in the morning and returned late at night; she barely ate or drank; and she shrivelled up like a blade of grass. People who knew her felt sorry for her, but behind her back they said different things; the lads stopped ogling her, and the girls stopped envying her. Sympathetic old women advised her to visit a sorcerer who lived across the Dnieper in a remote part of the forest: "He will tell you the whole truth and guide you on the right path to pursue!" Grief gives courage: Horpynka put her fear aside and set forth.

The autumn wind burst the waves on the Dnieper River and issued a muffled roar in the forest; yellow leaves fell from the trees and rustled as they whirled along the road; and the evening frowned upon the rainy sky, on the night Horpynka went to the sorcerer. No one knows what he told her; only that in vain did her mother wait for her all that evening, and in vain did her mother wait the next day, and on the third day – no one knew what happened to her! A few days later a fisherman from the monastery explained that when he was sailing in his boat, he had seen a young girl on the bank of the Dnieper: her face was scratched with tree needles and twigs, her hair messed up and her ribbons torn; but he did not dare to swim closer to her out of fear that it was either someone possessed or a wandering soul of the dead who had been a grave sinner.

The poor old woman cried her eyes out. At first light she would get up and wander far, far away, along both banks of the Dnieper, asking all who she encountered about her daughter and looking for her body on the sands of the riverbank. Every day, with grief and bitter tears, she made her lonely return home: there was no word about her sweet Horpynka! She took devout oaths and spent her remaining hard-earned money to sacrifice large candles to the Pechersk[26] Saints; for a time it brought some comfort to her heart, but the agony caused by the uncertainty of her daughter's fate never stopped. Autumn passed, and then the severe winter was also spent in a futile search, in tears and prayers. Reverend fathers, the monks of Kytaivska Pustyn, comforted the sorrowful mother and in their Christian way pitied the lost lamb; however, their compassion and consolatory talks could not erase the tragic loss from the mother's heart. As spring arrived, the old woman again began roaming the banks of the Dnieper, but still in vain. She wished to at least collect the bones of her poor Horpynka, bathe them with bitter tears and bury them, even if secretly[27], in the cemetery with other departed Orthodox worshippers. However, an evil fate had deprived her even of this last consolation.

The same sympathetic old women, who had urged the daughter to consult the sorcerer, encouraged the mother to seek help from him as well. In the words of the proverb, "He who is drowning is happy to clutch onto a razor." After some thought the old woman went into the forest. There, in a sinister cave or den, lived a sinister old man.

No one knew where he was from, when and how he came to the trans-Dnieper forest and how old he was; however, the old timers of Kyiv would recall that many years ago, as children, they heard from their grandparents about this sorcerer named Borovyk[28] , who was not known by any other name. When old Fenna, Horpynka's mother, came to the place where the stories said he could have been found, her hair stood on end and feverish trembling overcame her...

She saw an old man who was gnarled and wrinkled like some kind of revenant. On a hot May noon he lay on the bare ground under fur coats in the sun, but it seemed that he could not get warm. A circle had been drawn around the sorcerer, and at his feet sat a huge black toad, its big green eyes bulging. Behind the circle was a ball of every possible cold-blooded creature: vipers, snakes and lizards seethed and curled; large bats swayed on the branches of trees; while owls, eagle-owls and shrikes dozed on treetops and amongst the leaves. As soon as the old woman appeared, the toad suddenly croaked three times in a horrifying voice, bats beat their wings, eagle-owls and owls howled, and the snakes hissed, revealing their bloody fangs, and started writhing faster than ever. The old man raised himself a little, but on seeing the decrepit, timid woman, he waved a black cloth with some mysterious red silk insignia, and in a flash everything was gone – shouting, screeching, hissing and howling – except for the toad, which did not move from its spot and did not take its eyes off the sorcerer.

"Do not enter the circle," croaked the old man in a voice that was barely audible, as if it emanated from the grave. "And listen: you are crying and yearning for your daughter. Would you like to see her? Would you like to be with her again?"

"Oh, dear sir! How can I not wish it? She is my only child and is the apple of my eye."

"Listen then: I will give you a black boar tusk and black candle..."

Then he mumbled something in an unknown language, and the toad, having rotated its eyes, in one leap jumped into the dungeon, which was located a few steps from the circle. In another leap it jumped out, holding in its mouth a big white tusk and black candle; it put both objects in front of the old woman and sat back in its original spot.

"Soon Green Week[29] will arrive," the old man continued. "On the last day of this week, exactly at noon, go to the forest and find there a glade in the middle of the thicket. You will recognise it: there is not a blade of grass on it and large fern[30] bushes grow around it. Make your way to the glade, use a tusk to outline a circle around yourself and insert the black candle in the middle of the circle. Soon they will come running; you need to watch carefully, and as soon as you notice your daughter, grab her by the left arm and drag her into the circle. When the rest have finished running past, you take out the candle from the ground, then hold it in your hand while you lead your daughter to your house. Whatever she says, do not listen to her speeches but continue leading her, holding the candle over her head. Whatever happens afterwards, do not reveal it to your priests and monks, do not order any memorial services or prayers, just endure it for the whole year. Otherwise, you will be sorry..."

It seemed to the old woman that at that moment the toad cast a frightening sidelong look at her and clapped its ugly lips. Poor Fenna almost fell down from fright. As quickly as possible, she made a bow to the sorcerer, and, on her shaking legs, she doddered out from the forest. But is there anything that a mother's love cannot accomplish? The hope of finding her daughter reinforced the old woman's strength and gave her courage. On the last day of Green Week, when the sun was reaching noon, she went into the thicket of the forest and found there the glade described by the sorcerer. She drew a circle around herself with a black boar's tusk then stuck a black candle in the middle of the ground – and the candle illuminated itself, glowing with a blue light. Suddenly a noise broke out: a whooping and cheering. As fast as a whirlwind, a procession of countless young girls rushed across the glade. All of them were in light, transparent clothes, and all wore large wreaths that covered their hair completely and even came down to their shoulders. Some of them had made their wreaths from sedge, others from the twigs of the trees, so it seemed as if they had green hair. The girls ran, avoiding the circle and failing to notice or to see the old woman, and she forgot her fear and stared into the face of each of them. She saw it – here was her Horpynka, running. The old woman barely had time to grab her daughter by her left arm and pull her inside the circle. The others, apparently, failed to notice as they ran so fast and in such a frenzy, whooping and cheering as they swept past. The old Fenna hastily snatched the blazing black candle from the ground, held it over her daughter's head, and instantly the green sedge wreath crackled, caught fire and scattered in ashes from Horpynka's head. Inside the circle Horpynka stood as though frozen; but as soon as her mother led her out of the circle, she began to implore her in a soft and tender voice:

"Mother! Let me go to stroll in the forest, to play during the Green Week and then to dive back into our underwater homes... I know that you yearn for me and that you cry for me, but who is stopping you from being with me inseparably? Throw away your worthless fear and join us at the bottom of the Dnieper. It is fun there! It is easy there! Everyone becomes young there, and just as frisky as a trickle of water and just as playful and carefree as the young fish. Where we are, the sun shines brighter and the morning breeze breathes more freely. What is there in your land? Here, misery is all around – the hunger and the cold – but there we know no misery: we are content to splash in water, play with rainbows and look for gemstones at the river bottom and amuse ourselves with them. In winter we are warm under the ice as though under a fur coat; and in the summer, on a clear night, we go out to bask in the rays of the moon, amuse ourselves, have fun and often play tricks on the living. Is it so wrong if sometimes we tickle[31] people or take them to the bottom of the river? Are they worse off because of that? They become just as light and as free as we are... Mother! Let me go: I will suffer and suffocate among the living! Let me go, mother, if you love me..."

The old woman did not succumb, and she continued to lead her daughter to her house, but it was with great sorrow that she understood her daughter had become a *rusalka*. They came to the house, and the old woman took Horpynka inside. She sat opposite the stove, leaning with both arms on her knees and staring into the mouth of the stove. At that moment the black candle burnt down, and Horpynka became motionless. Her face turned blue, the limbs stiffened and became as cold as ice; her hair was wet, as if only now she had emerged from the water. It was horrible to look at her lifeless face, at her open, murky eyes that looked but did not see! Belatedly the old woman regretted that she had listened to the evil sorcerer; but even now her maternal feelings and some vague hope triumphed over her fear and any reproach of her conscience: she decided she would wait at any cost.

The day passed and night arrived, but Horpynka sat as before, dead and motionless. The old woman felt unnerved by the thought of spending the night with her horrifying guest, but, reluctantly, she stayed. Then the night passed, but Horpynka sat as before;

Detail of: *Vydubytskyi Monastery* by Mykhailo Sazhyn.

then days, weeks and months passed, but she sat motionlessly, leaning with her head on her arms, her eyes still open and murky, unvaryingly staring into the oven, and with her hair as wet as before. In the village rumours spread about it, and all the people, good and bad, did not dare to walk past the house, either during the day or the night; they all feared the revenant and feared old Fenna, who gained the notoriety of a witch. The path near the house was overgrown with grass and almost ceased to be visible; the neighbours went into the forest rarely and only as a last resort. Finally, the poor old woman gradually became accustomed to her misfortune and situation: already without fear she slept in the house, where the terrible guest sat entombed in her motionless state.

A year passed: the revenant continued to sit without making a movement or showing other signs of life. It was the time of Green Week once more. On the festival's first day, around noon, the old woman was cooking and had left the door of the house open. Suddenly, there was the sound of whooping and cheering and the rustling of rapid steps. Fenna shuddered and involuntarily looked at her daughter: Horpynka's face at once came to life; frightfully, as the blue colour disappeared, her eyes gleamed and a frenzied smile, as if intoxicated, flashed on her lips. She jumped up, clapped her hands three times and shouted: "Sisters, sisters, sisters!" and then, like lightening, she flew out after the noisy crowd... and disappeared without a trace!

The old woman, being tormented by her conscience, took a stringent vow: she joined a nunnery as a novice, undertaking the most difficult chores, praying incessantly and finally, having found peace in her soul, she died quietly, mourning her unfortunate daughter.

The following day, after the *rusalka* had escaped from her mother, they found a dead body in the forest. It was a Pole clothed in hunting attire, and his fellow countrymen identified him as Casimir Chepka, a clever young man who was the life of any party. His gun was loaded and lay beside him, but his dog was not with him; no wounds or signs of a violent death were found on his body, but his face was blue, and the veins were terribly strained. They knew that he had many friends and no obvious enemy. Doctors interpreted it as this and that, but the local folk explained the matter much more simply – they said that the deceased had been tickled to death by *rusalky*.

THE EVIL EYE

1833

I

Oh, kozak Mykyta's daughters were good, and kozak Mykyta was not a poor man himself. He had fourteen pairs of oxen with which to send *chumaky*[32] to the Don River to bring back fish or to the Crimea to bring back salt; and all his oxen were big, with sharp horns and wide foreheads, with strong backs and long-hanging woolly dewlaps. In the pasture kozak Mykyta grazed a herd of horses, the fastest and most valiant horses that ever existed. At home, kozak Mykyta had so many possessions that even in lean times a sprightly scribe would not be able to record them all. People also said that kozak Mykyta had treasure chests with so many ducats and silver that one could not carry it away, even with shovel.

II

Oh, kozak Mykyta's daughters were good: Halia with her jet-black eyebrows and Dokyika

43

with her rosy cheeks and Natalka with her fair face. Their father and mother instilled the fear of God in them. It was pleasing to the eye to watch them on summer Feast Days and on Sundays walking to Mass decorously and humbly, in delicate white *kuntushy*[33] with gored panels saffian boots with heel-tips, with their colourful head-ribbons dispersed over their shoulders, and lavish flowers of poppy, marigolds and periwinkle in their hair. All the lads stared at them and mumbled, scratching behind their ears: "Oh, they are terribly good daughters, and with a very rich father!"

III

Kozak Mykyta sat on a bench at the gate, smoking Romny[34] tobacco in a root pipe with a copper rim and watching God's earth; here he could see, on the road in the village outskirts, the dust spiralling high as a rider galloped headlong. Here, the rider flew into the village, nearer and nearer; the horse beneath him like a monster, as black as a raven's wing, smoke belching out from his nostrils as if from a distillery. Here, the rider reached kozak Mykyta and pulled on the reins, and the horse rested its hooves on the ground, arched its neck, lowered its head, whinnied and flashed with its unsteady eyes, so that it seemed to kozak Mykyta as if sparks flew in all directions.

IV

"Good day, good man!" said the traveller.

"Godspeed!" kozak Mykyta replied, having removed his pipe from his mouth and raised his hat. "Where is God sending you?"

It seemed to kozak Mykyta that the traveller twitched his moustache twice, and his horse snorted twice.

"I'm going far, far away: further than the eye can see and on foot further than a pair of shoes would last. But the point is this: where could I find lodgings for the night?"

"You are welcome here! We are pleased to see good people. God always sends a man his daily bread."

Silently, the traveller dismounted his horse, led it by its reins, tied them to a pole under a covering, then entered the house with kozak Mykyta.

V

The traveller was not attractive: his face was pallid, without a drop of blood in it; his nose was big like an onion; the lips were puckered; tufts of messy ginger moustache stuck out on either side of his face; the same ginger eyebrows hung down like dense bristles, obscuring his eyes so that they were completely invisible; and ginger-red *oseledets*[35] lay like a strip of dried blood along his temple and curled behind his ear. *I will say it again*: the traveller was not attractive! By the look of him, he was neither old nor young; his peculiar sour grimace instead of a smile and his deep voice, which erupted from his throat as though it emanated from the grave, promised nothing good about him. He wore a *zhupan*[36] made from fine cloth and a Turkish knife, with a silver handle decorated with precious gems that burnt like smouldering coals, which was stuck behind his Persian sash. Without saying the Lord's Prayer, as is customary among the Orthodox, and having barely nodded to the mistress of the house and their daughters, he sat down at the table without any courtesy and sprawled out as though he were in a tavern.

VI

"Good man, I see, you are one of the *Zaporizhian*[37] kozaks?" kozak Mykyta asked him.

"It may be," was the answer.

"How long have you been gallivanting about with the other kozaks?"

"Well, for donkey's years."

"And what should I call you?"

"Lavro Khorobyt."

"What do you think: did you lay many of the infidel heads to rest in your time?"

"All sorts of things used to happen; let them lie."

"And did you have to travel far to war at times?"

"Yes, I did; no jackdaws from your village reach there."

"And have you endured many labours?"

"Even a good pair of oxen would not be able to carry them."

"On occasions the seasoned *chumaky* have described the vastness of the infidels' lands! What prosperous places! Is there anything that is not born there?"

"Blue are the hills that are far from us."

"And what evil tribes those Turks and Tatars are!"

"There are Christians who are no better than they are."

Kozak Mykyta realised that his guest would not submit to questioning, and that not one worthwhile word could be dragged out of him. He looked askance at the traveller and went silent.

VII

At dinner, through his hanging eyebrows, the traveller coveted kozak Mykyta's pretty daughters, just like a pike that, through the reeds, covets the small frisky fish; however, the beauties heard neither greeting, nor any other word from him. He sat sullenly and, puffing, sipped kozak Mykyta's *zapikanka*[38] and *ternivka*[39]. When he occasionally glanced at one of the girls, she involuntarily lowered her eyes, not out of shame but out of fear: the beauties were frightened by the stares of the invisible eye that glowed faintly behind the thick ginger eyebrows. The guest got up from the table in the same manner that he sat down: neither praying to God, nor saying a good word to the hosts. What kind of a person was he? Everyone thought it and wondered about it, but no one could find out.

VIII

The whole night long a dog howled under the window, and the beauties felt choked up and terrified. They could not sleep and constantly tossed in bed, and if for a moment they dozed off, then terrifying dreams instantly interrupted their sleep. One moment they heard funeral lamentations and bells chiming for the dead; another moment the strange guest looked at them with such eyes that the cold clutched their chests, took their breath away and fettered their muscles in ice. The beauties thrashed about, moaned through their deep sleep and woke up in terror, and in the morning they got up with heavy heads and disconcerted spirits.

A Ukrainian Woman from Chernihiv by Opanas Slastion.

IX

"Listen, kozak Mykyta," Khorobyt said to his host in the morning at breakfast, "betroth your ebony-browed daughter Halia to me."

"My daughter Halia is already betrothed. Her fiancé is from a good family and is a well-to-do man; and whosoever without a cause denies a groom his engaged bride will be punished by God."

"Then give me your rosy-cheeked Dokyika."

"My daughter Dokyika also has exceptional suitors. With God's help, as one daughter goes down the aisle, we will hand out *rushnyky*[40] for the other one."

"Well, then at least fair-faced Natalka..."

"My daughter Natalka is a young child and knows nothing yet. How can I give her away to such distant lands?"

"Kozak Mykyta, you have denied me. You rejected my proposal to marry your daughter. Watch that you do not regret it later."

"What will be, will be; and that will be what God commands!" replied kozak Mykyta.

X

Without uttering another word, Lavro Khorobyt went to saddle his raven horse, which was whinnying and snorting and beating the ground with its hooves. At that moment kozak Mykyta's three daughters entered the house. They left their chambers thinking that the passing guest had already galloped off and was not coming back. But here he was, walking proudly and with dignity, jingling his silver and gold coins.

"It's for you, host, for your lodging and kindness," he said, having put his hand into his pocket and pulled out a handful of silver coins.

"This is not an inn or tavern," kozak Mykyta replied disconcerted, "we offer our guests what God has sent, and we do not take money for *bread and salt*[41] from anybody."

"Then allow me to gift your daughters with something to remember me by!" said Khorobyt, and, having put his hand into his pocket again, he pulled out a handful of golden trinkets. The girls were dazzled by the rings, earrings, expensive necklaces and buckles. These were of all sorts of styles, colours and value! Some glowed like smouldering coals, others shone like a cat's eyes at night, while on others rainbows beamed brighter than those that reach down from heaven to earth and drink water from streams and wells. The young women admired the expensive trinkets, exchanging glances with each other, and giving sidelong glimpses at their father. Whatever happened to their fear of the traveller?

"Take it, if the good man gives it as a gift to remember him by," said their father. "It is a gift, not a payment."

XI

"You, ebony-browed Halia, begin!" said Lavro Khorobyt. "Come closer and choose what you fancy."

Halia came up, stretched her hand towards the table, looked at Khorobyt, then screamed and jumped aside, as if she had stepped on a snake.

"How shy she is!" the traveller commented, laughing. "Let it be so; if you do not want these, let rosy-cheeked Dokyika choose."

Dokyika came closer, looked at the gifts and at the guest, and then also screamed and jumped aside in the same instant.

"So, this is how it is! As one does, the other follows," said Khorobyt with the same laugh. "Your turn, fair-faced Natalka!"

And Natalka moved forward timidly, inadvertently looked at the traveller, screamed and almost fell. It appeared to her that Khorobyt's ginger eyebrows were raised on end like spines on a hedgehog, and, like jets, two thin threads of sharp, burning and deadening light from his pale gray eyes poured on her. It caused a shiver to run through the body, fear to settle in one's soul and longing to dig into one's heart. This is what the evil eye is: it takes a look at the green forest, and the green forest withers!

XII

"Well, thanks for your 'bread and salt'; I will remember it, and you will not forget me either, even though your daughters turned shy and did not take my gifts," declared Lavro Khorobyt, regarding the girls with a stare the devil uses to look at the human soul. And they, poor things, stood with their arms crossed, and their whole bodies trembled.

"Farewell," he muttered. "Remember me kindly!" And he laughed so that everyone's heart went cold. In a trice, he dashed behind the door, mounted his horse and vanished into thin air.

XIII

"Mama! I feel so miserable and sorrowful!" said ebony-browed Halia.

"Mama! Cold shivers run up and down my spine, my hands and feet are as if in ice, but inside it is burning," said rosy-cheeked Dokyika. Ah! But already she was as white as a sheet.

"Mama! My head is bursting with pain, everything is spinning, and it becomes darker and darker in my eyes," said fair-faced Natalka.

"Save us, save us, Mama!" all three repeated. "Save us from the wicked man! Call a *znakhar*[42]. Let him break the hex of the evil eye!"

But all in vain! Neither the *znakhar*, nor anyone else helped: the further away Lavro Khorobyt rode, the worse the beauties' condition became. With the arrival of sunset the light left their bright eyes too... At night the pious old women gathered in the light of the wax candles to sit at a wide table, on which the three deceased lay under a white shroud. Plaintively, the sexton read psalms over them. Their father and mother could barely breathe with their anguish and sorrow.

XIV

A big chapel stands in the cemetery on the outskirts of the village; there are three crosses on the chapel and a high and wide grave under the chapel. Kozak Mykyta's three daughters are buried in that grave. Good people, when passing by, cross themselves and pray: "Send, Lord, eternal rest and eternal memory of the deceased." After that, they involuntarily would add: "And let there be no good on earth and in heaven to the wicked man, who with his snake eye withered and ended the lives of three beautiful fresh and lush flowers!"

WANDERING LIGHT

1832

A warrior flew upon his horse towards Kyiv. The warrior's armour was blue, and his sword of bulat steel dangled from a silver chain, hitting hard on the ribs of the spirited horse, his loyal companion. The warrior was returning home, not from the magnificent feast of a Kniaz[43], but from a feast that was bloody, where on the bodies of the Kassoges[44] his sharp sword had inscribed in deep veins his name – Velesyl.

A warrior flew upon his horse towards Kyiv. There his faithful and beautiful bride Mylava awaited him. It had been a long time since the warrior and the young maiden exchanged their rings: the dangerous war was the only force that was able to separate the two hearts, which burned with the pure flames of the pre-wedding feast torches.

But what was that blue twinkle, which flashed as it moved in the misty haze with a shimmering glow? The warrior protected himself by making the sign of the cross, believing that it was a spirit, the tempter of

Detail of: *Off to War* by Mykola Pymonenko.

travellers; however, the light did not disappear and only moved further and further as Velesyl approached.

"If you are a spirit, then disappear; if you are sorcerer, then display your evil power in a fight with me!" exclaimed the warrior, who valiantly set off in pursuit of the deceptive light. His spirited horse snorted, jumped over the fence, and carried the warrior over the graves, and yet the blue twinkle kept flitting from one grave to another, continually eluding the warrior.

Forlorn was the place where the warrior rode then – it was a settlement of the dead, a peaceful cemetery. Finally, the blue twinkle began to glow steadily on one grave. The warrior rushed there... It was a fresh grave, and the trampled turf had not yet had time to grow up into a velvety carpet. Suddenly the blue twinkle disappeared, and thick darkness enveloped the surroundings.

The warrior's horse snorted and, having lowered its head, beat the ground with a hoof. A yearning premonition clawed into his zealous heart; the warrior said: "It is not something good that you are foreboding, my bold horse, my loyal friend. You do not yearn in anticipation of joy, my poor heart! It seems that here lies the end to my path; it seems that here all my joy is buried."

Having dismounted his horse the warrior leaned to the grave cross as if it was presenting all that was dear to him in his life. The horse stood as before, with its head bowed, and it drummed the ground with its hooves. For a long while sad thoughts followed one after another in Velesyl's soul; eventually, a gentle sleep fell upon his eyelids.

And he saw: from the paradise porch, from the evergreen gardens, Mylava's face appeared, glowing with the dawn of immortality. With a warm, heavenly smile Mylava beckoned her groom... And suddenly, a terrible thunder broke out in the air and fell in a fiery stream, interrupting his reverie. The horse reared, but the warrior sat, motionless.

A quiet morning shone brightly after the stormy night. People came to the cemetery to pay their last respects to their departed brethren. They found the corpse of Velesyl on the grave of the beautiful Mylava.

Kupalo Eve

1831

Warrior Konchyslav rode through the night along the banks of the Dnieper River; from far-off campaigns he was making his return to the grand city of Kyiv, to the court of his glorious ruler, gracious Kniaz Volodymyr[45].

The bright moon rolled across the dark blue sky and its pale yellow rays reflected on Konchyslav's knightly armour. The warrior was deep in thought. At the time he left the capital city and the court of glorious Volodymyr, the people of Kyiv believed in Perun[46], Kupalo[47], Veles[48] and the Golden Baba[49]; but now, while he was in foreign lands, the news reached him that the Slavic idols had been smashed and drowned, and that there were now temples to the Living God, and crosses shining on the golden domes of Kyiv. A sinful doubt and contemptuous pride crept into the soul of the warrior. He thought: "Even if the Kniaz and all the people of Kyiv have betrayed their old gods, then Konchyslav alone will remain faithful to them."

The bright moon rolled across the dark blue sky and its pale yellow rays glided over

The Kozak on his Way to the Sich by Lev Zhemchuzhnykov.

white canvas tents, which were spread around one cheerful valley where Konchyslav's path lay. Noise, songs, *husli*[50] sounds and the nightingale-like whistles of flutes echoed far across the valley. The warrior prompted his trusty steed and galloped towards the jubilant crowd. White shadowy figures flashed in front of him, to the side of the tents and in front of the brightly burning bonfires.

As the warrior arrived, a whole string of beautiful girls ran up to him and grabbed him by his hands. The girls, one more beautiful than the other, one more charming than the other, surrounded the warrior and sweetly beseeched him to dismount his horse and rejoice with them. The prettiest, the most playful and the most affable girl jumped out of the *khorovod*[51] and, like a bird, flew up to the warrior. She grabbed his hand and said:

"Brave and mighty warrior, tonight is Kupalo Eve[52]! We all uphold our old faith and came here from the capital, Kyiv, to jump freely over burning bonfires and to commemorate our god through dances. We know, warrior Konchyslav, that you are also one of us: all the warriors except you have betrayed the faith of their fathers. Dismount your horse and celebrate with us!"

The warrior dismounted nimbly, and, with cheerful shouts and squeals, the other girls took away his horse. Konchyslav was left eye-to-eye with the affable stranger; the warrior's handsome eyes lit up with the fire of desire; his mighty chest heaved up and down from excitement; and his heart threatened to break out of its banks. Walking hand-in-hand with the beauty and leaning upon her white shoulder, he asked in a pleasing voice:

"What is your name, beautiful maiden?"

"My name is Nasoloda[53]," she answered, with such a look and a smile that fire ran through the warrior's blood and veins, and its burning flame scorched his heart.

The young women did not return. Only Konchyslav and Nasoloda were left together, jumping over the fire in front of the Kupalo idol. The lovely maiden's playfulness and laughter completely charmed the warrior. Suddenly, the beauty, having grabbed him by his hand and looked at him with a passionate and heart-wrenching smile, pointed at one of the tents and ran there quickly, as lightly and gracefully as a gazelle. The warrior ran after her, caught up with her at the entrance of the tent, embraced the young woman's supple figure with his arm, and, woven together in a tender embrace, they disappeared under the white and rippling roof of the tent.

"Why are your kisses so cold, sweet beauty?" asked Konchyslav, coming to his senses after the first surge of intoxication. "They shower upon my heart as if made from ice."

Nasoloda just laughed in reply and gently tickled the warrior.

"It is damp and cold here," he said again. "A deadly shiver strikes me to the bone."

Nasoloda laughed louder and louder and tickled the warrior harder and harder.

"No, this is intolerable!" cried out Konchyslav, trying to escape from the beauty's embrace. "Even on the very day of Koliada[54] I never suffered such excruciating chills!"

At that moment something rustled and stirred around the tent. The warrior looked up... Grey, foamy waves swirled violently above him. There was no tent any longer, and only coils of white foam curled at the place where previously the canvas had fluttered in the night's first breeze... The warrior looked at Nasoloda... in front of him sat a malevolent *rusalka* grinning insidiously, whose long green hair fell like a mossy silk upon her pallid, bare shoulders and breasts, which were as cold as the eternal ice of the Caucasus. Suddenly, she burst into a loud, frantic laughter once more; and in an instant waves came gushing more fiercely than ever before and pressed against Konchyslav, smothering his breath, getting tighter and tighter... until they completely consumed the warrior, who in his soul rejected the welcoming calls of Piety.

God's Fool

1827

A young officer rode along merrily from a nearby village, where he had spent a day in the most pleasant company – the company of hospitable hosts, their lovely daughters and five or six of his young friends. He hurried to return to the town before nightfall because he knew he ought to be on guard duty the next day. The moon, a faithful companion of the Ukrainian summer nights, was scattering its silver light onto the groves, hills and fields, and it painted charming pictures before his eyes, which were complemented by his vivid imagination.

The dashing horses carried the officer's coach rapidly. Suddenly, at the turn near a ravine, something black, lying almost on the very road, flashed before the eyes of the easily frightened horses. The horses jerked, rushed forward and, ignoring the coachman's reins, dashed to the side of the road, across the ruts and bumps. The coachman fell off his seat, the officer followed him almost immediately, and the horses soon disappeared from view.

Feeling no injury, Melskyi – that was the officer's name – stood up, dusted himself off, and went searching for his coachman, whom he soon found also on his feet and in good health. Both of them had fallen on the soft soil and suffered only an accidental fall. It was too late to look for the horses – and where would they find them? The officer, with all the carefreeness of his young age, left his horses and chariot at the mercy of fate and decided to uncover what was the cause of their fright.

"Ivan," he addressed his coachman, who was walking behind him, "what do you think frightened the horses?"

"I beg your pardon, sir, but how can one not be frightened: there was a whole pack of wolves on the road!"

"Coward! No wonder they say that the hundred eyes of fear see danger everywhere."

"Truly, sir, there were at least two or three pairs of them."

"Stop talking nonsense. Do you really think that if they were wolves, they would not have fled the moment we swept past them so loudly?"

"As you wish, sir, but I saw half a dozen eyes that glowed like coal."

"Enough, enough! You saw some firefly in the grass or nothing at all. Follow me: let us go and find out what it was."

"But how, sir!? I have neither axe, nor the big wrench I use for the wheels: everything was left behind in the coach."

"You have your whip with you, and I can see a large folding knife behind your belt: this is very satisfactory. Follow me, and not another word."

Not daring to disobey his master, Ivan followed him, holding both of his weapons in his two hands, with his head hanging low and muttering something under his breath.

Taking precautions, Melskyi also drew his sword and was examining the road ahead of him. It took little effort to find the black monster that had frightened Ivan and the horses. It was a man. He was lying on the edge of the road, having bent his legs under his robe and wrapped his head with his arm, and seemed to sleep soundly.

"Get up, you drunk," Melskyi shouted, kicking him in his ribs with the toe of his boot.

"Drunk? I am no drunk. Those are your eyes that are intoxicated," a rough, hoarse voice replied.

"Get up then, unless you want to be lifted by force."

"Leave me alone! You envy me because I am here sleeping in the open field, and you also had the desire to lie on the damp ground. But wait a week; then I, in turn, will interrupt you..."

"Well, as you wish, my friend, but I will sober you up," Melskyi said, mistaking him for a drunk, who was delirious from a hangover... "Ivan, lift him!"

"Do not touch me, brute!" the alleged drunk said and rose quickly to his feet.

He was a tall man with a stubbly beard and messy hair. His face was pallid and in the moonlight it had appeared to be lifeless. His cloudy, wandering eyes showed that his head was not in the healthiest state.

"Ah, this is our half-wit," the coachman exclaimed, regaining his senses after the fright. "In the town, they call him Stupid Vasyl."

"Stupid!" Vasyl repeated, mimicking the coachman. "It is true, Vasyl does not abuse the poor horses or sell their hay and oats on the side, does not hit his poor billygoat for no reason, does not go to the inn at night and does not besmirch his master behind his back. Vasyl is God-fearing, goes to church, reads prayers and sings the stichera; Vasyl lives on alms and God forbid he steals or cheats."

During the whole speech the coachman was not himself and, having lowered his head, fixed his eyes on the ground as if looking for something under his feet. Meanwhile, Melskyi smiled and looked at the coachman and at the half-wit, who stood without a hat, in a long black robe made from thick cloth and sewn like a monastic cassock; he was girdled by a narrow belt with a rusty iron buckle; he wore no footwear at all, and in his hands he held a long stick with patterns carved in its bark.

"Ivan," Melskyi addressed his coachman, "go in the direction where the horses ran away and try to find them!"

"Go!" uttered God's Fool. "You will find them but will not take them; they will respond but will not give in."

The coachman went looking for the horses while Melskyi went on the road towards the town. The half-wit followed him without falling behind, making long, quick steps, waving and leaning on his walking stick, and singing spiritual songs. He did not engage in any conversations with Melskyi.

Melskyi was brought up in the present century and according to this century's customs and, consequently, without any prejudice.

However, his strange companion was instilling some unfamiliar feeling in him: it was neither superstitious fear nor suspicion, but something in between the two. The half-wit's rough and hoarse voice and the gloomy tunes of his hymns of lament tormented the young officer's hearing and spread an incomprehensible yearning through his soul.

During the whole journey Vasyl sang and did not speak a word; Melskyi was also silent, as if he was afraid to start a conversation with him. In this manner, they reached the town outpost. The sentry called out to them and then, having seen Melskyi's uniform and face, respectfully let him pass; but, as one could notice in the bright moonlit night, the soldier seemed surprised at the sight of his regiment's officer on foot and with such a strange companion.

"Your honour," the soldier said in a low voice, after approaching Melskyi, "would you command me to detain this tramp? Sometimes he passes back and forth through the outpost twenty times a night, and God knows what his business is here and whether all the intentions on his mind are good ones?"

"A tramp!" said the half-wit loudly. "But would you have detained the tramp who once absented himself without permission from his regiment and then was dragged back in by the neck? He needs to feel some rods... and many, many of them! Fortunately, his commander is kind and had pity on his back."

The soldier was dumbfounded, and Melskyi looked at God's Fool with surprise. It seemed uncanny to him – how could a man deprived of the full use of his mind know all the secrets belonging to people who were strangers to him?

The half-wit, having finished his speech, continued walking along the street with his usual stride. Melskyi soon caught up with him; whether out of curiosity or because of some other impulse he decided to speak to him.

"Where do you live?" he asked the half-wit.

"Under the sky on the ground" Vasil replied curtly.

"I believe you. But where is your home?"

"It is not here, but there!" said God's Fool, raising his stick and drawing a half-circle in the air.

"Where are you lodging for the night?"

"Where God takes me."

"Then stay a night at my place. I will feed you..."

61

"Yes, you will!" God's Fool interrupted him abruptly. "Today is Friday, and there is either a chicken or a duck on your table."

"Very well. I will arrange to give you some Lenten food; we will provide you with fine wine and a good bed."

"Vasyl drinks water. Vasyl sleeps on the bare ground or on the floor. Have it your way: whatever happens, happens – I will spend the night at your place."

Neither Melskyi nor God's Fool spoke another word until they reached the officer's accommodation. Dressed as a batman, Melskyi's servant opened the door at the sound of his master knocking and almost dropped the candle taking a step back when he saw what guest his master had brought home with him.

"Vasyl is not the devil!" God's Fool said hurriedly. "He wanders at night but does not loaf about. At the shops he does not put anything on others' accounts."

The crafty servant decided to play dumb. He grinned and turned around to light the stairs for his master.

"Laugh!" God's Fool grumbled, as if to himself. "You will cry, and you will cry bitterly, and at the same time of the night."

Melskyi looked at God's Fool, but he was already whispering something else, evidently prayers because from time to time he crossed himself and bowed his head.

"Cheerfully, brightly and beautifully!" he said, entering the room. "A lot of money, a lot!"

And he began singing an old song about the prodigal son:

Oh, woe to me, a true sinner.
Woe to me, who knows no good deeds.

On Melskyi's orders, the dinner for God's Fool was prepared, but he ate only bread and drank water and very little wine. During the dinner he was silent, and only sometimes made some pious comments. Then, he prayed to God, thanked the owner, and said, "Now let me sleep close to the entrance door. When it is time for me to go, I will wake someone from your staff and that person will lock the door behind me. You will see me again, and again, and again; then Vasyl will say 'great thanks' to you and go far, far away, somewhere you cannot see from here!"

He chose a place in the entrance hall and lay on the floor near the door. Melskyi stopped and watched to see what he would do next. God's Fool prayed long and with fervent faith, kneeling, then often raising his arms to the sky. Next, he placed a pillow given to him upon the floor under his head and threw aside the rest of the bedlinen. He lay down without undressing and momentarily shut his eyes.

Melskyi went to his bedroom and climbed into bed. He thought that tiredness from the country parties and dances, as well as his unplanned long walk, would ensure him a deep and peaceful sleep, but he was wrong. The strange look of his strange guest, his words, which partly unveiled what had happened and what would happen in the future, did not leave the young officer's mind. He tried his best to convince himself that the half-wit's words were the typical consequence of a deranged mind, that although it appeared that he hinted about matters he could not possibly know, he was really taking random guesses, knowing the servants' usual habits, and that whatever he said to the soldier he could have somehow heard from his comrades – nonetheless, God's Fool appeared in his visions constantly. Several times Melskyi shut his eyes and forced himself to sleep; but he felt so choked up, the room was smothering him, as if its walls were closing in around his bed and the ceiling above him was bending to the floor. To his annoyance, Melskyi was tossing around and blaming himself for this weakness that was previously unknown to him, and closing his eyes time after time; but even if he sometimes sank into oblivion as if before a sleep, the image of God's Fool, his pallid sunken cheeks, his grim eyes and his tall stature, which grew taller and taller until finally God's Fool turned into a giant, remained relentlessly in the young officer's dreams and tortured him like a fever's delirium. He had visions that God's Fool was grabbing his arm with his sinewy hand or that he was leaning over his head and saying in a rough and hoarse voice: "Get up, I came to interrupt your rest." Melskyi would wince and jump up. Finally, seeing that he could not force himself to sleep, he got up, sat on the bed and started to sort his thoughts in order to find the natural cause of his insomnia and the bizarre dreams that troubled him. "Fine," he said to himself eventually. "There is nothing unnatural: the excessive movements today excited my blood; it is a temporary fit of nerves. It's peculiar, I'm a soldier and feared neither bullets nor bayonets, but I upset my imagination with some absurd delirium – and how? With some half-wit!" Deliberating this way, Melskyi calmed himself down; but to completely reassure himself that God's Fool was no threat, he stood up, took a lit night candle from the other room and went to the entrance hall. For a while he stared at the strange culprit of his sleeplessness. God's Fool was sound asleep, his face reflecting the peacefulness of his clear conscience and childlike carelessness; only once while dreaming did he wave his hand in front of his face from side to side, as if chasing away something unpleasant. Melskyi returned to his bedroom and lay down in bed again. This time nature took its toll, and he started to fall asleep, when suddenly he heard something crackling over his head, as if the walls had collapsed and were falling with a long rumble. He jumped up again and, instead of his dreams, he attributed this to some noise in the house. Again he took the candle and walked through all the rooms and looked at God's Fool, who slept as before, while everyone else in Melskyi's household was also immersed in a deep sleep – it was peaceful and quiet in the house and all the silver and other objects were safe in their places. After his examination Melskyi went back to his room and this time slept quietly until the moment when his servant came to remind him that it was time to get ready to go on guard.

"What about our odd-fellow from yesterday?" Melskyi asked.

"He left, sir, far before the sunrise. Dawn had barely begun when he woke me up to lock the door after him, and told me to only report to you that soon he would say 'a great thank you' for your bread and salt."

"Is everything safe in the house?" Melskyi asked, trying to avoid directly enquiring about the noise that had woken him at night.

"Everything is fine, sir," replied the servant, almost through his clenched teeth, assuming that this question was related to Vasyl. "This fool never steals where he lodges for a day or a night; it does not matter if something lies in temptation's way."

"That is not what I asked about," said Melskyi, and rephrased his question: "Has the coachman returned and were the horses found?"

"The coachman arrived, sir, but without horses. He is here, in the entrance hall, waiting for you to see him."

Melskyi sent for the coachman, who then told him that in a small grove he had heard the neighing and braying of the horses but, because of the darkness due to the moon waning, because of the thicket and fallen trees, he could not get to them; that fear of the wolves prevented him from waiting there until the morning, but that now he was going there again.

Detail of: *A View of Podil, Kyiv,* by Vasyl Shternberg.

Having reproached the coachman and sent him away, Melskyi dressed, went into another room and looked out the window. There he watched his horses racing at full speed with the coach down the street and then suddenly stopping in front of his house. God's Fool drove them boldly and skilfully, and the coachman ran after them. Having stopped the horses at full speed, God's Fool handed the reins to the coachman, who had caught up with them, and then went into Melskyi's room.

"My trouble, though not my fault," said the visitor. "Vasyl fixed things as best as he could. Here are your horses and chariot. Some things got broken and others got lost. But do not grieve; you have plenty of extra roubles, so many that you can throw them through a window! Which you are practically doing."

"How do you know that?" Melskyi asked him.

"I know. I know! Vasyl knows everything since this is his fate. The colourful gaming cards pull many roubles across the green cloth; then there are also feasts, entertainments, and God knows what else! It is true: you give *hryvni*[55] to the poor, and a lot... Fine, fine, not all will be lost!"

"Here is a *hryvnia* for you as well, for finding and bringing my horses," said Melskyi, handing him a gold coin.

"Thank you! It is lovely, lovely! Many candles to God and many *hryvni* to the brothers," responded God's Fool, holding the gold coin in his palm and looking at it. "Thank you and farewell!"

Melskyi wanted him to stay longer, but he had already gone; a servant who was sent after him called him on the street, but he did not look back and walked away, taking wide swift steps and singing a sticheron.

Nothing special happened to Melskyi for the rest of the day or during the following days; he had almost forgotten about God's Fool, who no longer either visited or was encountered. On the sixth day, in the evening, he was getting ready for a ball being held by the rich and opulent Countess Verska. He was already taking a seat in his coach to ride to the countess, when he saw Vasyl, who was walking down the street and waving his stick, giving him the sign to wait. Melskyi, wishing to know what was happening, ordered the coachman to halt.

"Wait. Turn back your horses," said God's Fool approaching the officer. "Stay away from there; it is crowded and stuffy there; everything is spinning there − feet and heads. As soon as you start spinning, you forget yourself; one thing is in your heart, but another thing is on your tongue. Our tongue is our enemy: it runs before our wit."

Melskyi smiled and, consumed by anticipation of the amusement that awaited, threw a few silver coins to God's Fool and shouted to the coachman: "Go!" Soon after they rode down the street. But then, turning into another street, with an involuntary movement he looked back and saw God's Fool standing in the same spot, looking at the sky and swinging his arms apart, as if saying: "Thy will be done!"

In the roar of the festivities Melskyi soon forgot the unpleasant impression left by the sudden appearance, words and expressive gestures of God's Fool. He was exceptionally cheerful and jocular and did an extraordinary amount of dancing. Among all the girls there whose beauty adorned the ball, Sofia Lastynska, an eighteen-year old beauty, a rich bachelorette and the best dancer in the town, was the one who stood out the most. Sofia was well mannered, intelligent and had a kind heart; however, all these good qualities were overshadowed by her coquetry, levity or, rather, her careless and uncontrollable inclination to wag her tongue at someone else's expense. Melskyi possessed the same weakness, and that is why at all the balls where they happened to be together, either during dancing or in between the dances, they always found an opportunity to exchange caustic remarks at the expense of other dancers. Sometimes, glancing at the card tables, they talked about the funny old women and argumentative old men who sat there. Often Melskyi's sarcastic smirk or Sofia's careless and loud laughter exposed, to others, what those two were saying to each other softly, and, often rightly, provincial sensitivity led many to think that whatever was said was on their account. In turn, the vengeful pride of the ridiculed or of those who believed that they were ridiculed, labelled the pair 'inseparable'. Indeed, while making a mockery of others, Sofia failed to pay attention to her own behaviour: she did not notice how often and incautiously she was looking for Melskyi among other dancers or how often she sat further from the others in order to reserve a seat for him beside herself. Melskyi was not one of those self-obsessed young men who would interpret any trivial gesture from a pretty woman as a sign she favoured him; however, such an obvious disposition as Sofia's towards him did not escape his observant eye; he also felt some attraction towards her – Sofia was young, beautiful, educated, with a lively passionate mind... However, due to the strange contrariness of their hearts' inclinations, their whole relationship was limited to their mutual willingness to mock others. Melskyi's heart was as yet silent or still searching for other qualities in Sofia that were better than those he had come to know as a result of their social acquaintance.

It is easy to guess that at the Countess Verska's ball this inseparable couple soon found each other. For several dances in a row they were indeed inseparable, and the envious youth and those of resentful pride whispered among themselves and predicted their imminent wedding. As often happens, while ridiculing others they did not notice that they themselves were ridiculed. Towards the end of the ball the guests began to pair up for the cotillion; Melskyi was near Sofia, and, thanks to the long-lasting figures of the endless dance, their sharp comments floated in complete freedom from one to the other and vice versa.

"Here is the biggest beauty," Sofia was saying, glancing at one of the dancers, "at least as far as her height is concerned. Would you have at least one grenadier at your regiment who, in his shako and at full stretch, could reach her?"

"But what a tiny suitor she has," responded Melskyi. "He reaches her waist precisely. Look at how the poor thing torments his feet trying to keep up with her in a waltz. But wise nature always loves an equation: the measure of the two together constitutes a complete pair of medium-height dancers."

"Oh, look, look at those yellow-grey eyes: how enticingly they spin under the white eyelashes! The poor things, they imagine that someone can find them attractive!"

"And, apparently, they were not mistaken. Look how this long-legged German, that lady's suitor, fawns over her. Bravo! He tells her flattering things; you can see it in the pathetic expression of his eyes and face."

"Have a good look at that Firebird. There are crimson flowers on her head, a crimson dress, a crimson blush on her cheeks and almost crimson hair! Certainly she, *par excellence*, deserves the Russian epithet: 'the Red Maiden'."

"And her poor suitor, the oaf warrior. Indubitably, the waltz seems to him a funeral march; he frowns so and makes such a sulky physiognomy."

Listening to her and making comments too, Melskyi noticed that Sofia, laughing at his jokes with a very important air, sometimes looked back. There, a few steps away, stood an artillery officer, holding his finger to his mouth as if chewing on his nails, and sternly looking at Melskyi and Sofia in turn. Everything comes to an end; and the cotillion, which sometimes lasts until morning, especially in the provinces, this time ended fairly soon. Sofia disappeared from Melskyi's eyes, and he, wanting to get some fresh air, went to the glass doors leading to the garden. There, the artillery officer, who apparently was waiting for him, blocked his way.

"I beg your pardon," said Melskyi quite politely.

"Let me firstly inquire, dear sir, what your young lady was saying and why she was laughing."

"That is good!" Melskyi responded, not yet losing his patience. "Was that lady entrusted in your custody? But even if so, I hope that you know that the laws of chivalry..."

"Dear sir!" The artillery officer interrupted him dispassionately. "I demand from you not idle talk, but deeds..."

"And I demand from you, sir," said Melskyi picking up on his tone, "to tell me where did you get the right to interrogate me?"

"I will show you that alright – when the time comes."

"Whereas I will show you how I can deal with meddling interrogators."

"Impudent!"

One word led to another and their rattle became louder and louder; a group of curious spectators gathered around the two officers. Everyone asked what the dispute was about. But neither Melskyi nor the artillery officer could, or wanted to, divulge the root cause of the quarrel.

As always, and in this case as well, there were helpful conciliators and ardent instigators on both sides. Melskyi's comrades insisted that for the sake of the honour of their uniform the matter had to end in a duel, explicitly a duel to the death[56]; the defenders of the artillery officer echoed his words. Both opponents sought and wanted the same. Immediately, they went into the garden and appointed: the seconds and witnesses; the place of the duel – in the grove on the second mile from the town; the weapons – pistols; a fight to death or a very serious injury; and a time – the following day, at seven o'clock in the morning.

There were no roads back to reconciliation; there was no opportunity to explain or for a guilty party to apologise to the right party: everything was agreed upon and arranged. Fortunately, the women only knew that there was a dispute, but out of precaution they were not told, why, for what reason and how it ought to come to an end.

Both opponents immediately left the ball with their seconds and witnesses. Sofia's eyes looked for Melskyi and, failing to find him, she wondered about his early departure: she did not even suspect that she, unintentionally although not entirely innocently, was the reason why he had to expose his chest to the bullets.

Once at home, Melskyi sat at his writing desk and decided not to go to bed. He called his servant, ordered him to bring his pistols, examined them, then chose and loaded the bullets. However, nature was taking its toll: the situation, so to speak, was falling from his hands; the bullets fell to the floor, and the gunpowder poured past the bullets. His extreme absent-mindedness or, more accurately, the absence of any extraneous thoughts, except for the upcoming duel, would have been obvious to eyes even less inquisitive than those of Ihnatiy, his servant.

At first glance upon his master's arrival, Ihnatiy had noticed a change in his face. Curt orders, which were continually repeated and then cancelled, his changed voice, the request for pistols and bullets – all that helped the astute servant to unravel the terrible truth. He did not dare ask his master about that; but because he was accustomed from a very young age to be with him and, despite his minor mischiefs, being genuinely devoted to his master, he went out to the hall and wept bitterly.

At this moment a loud knock was heard at the entrance door. Ihnatiy jerked, and coldness scattered through his whole body; however, he went and opened the door to see who was knocking: it was God's Fool.

"Vasyl told you precisely a week ago: 'You will cry' – and cry you must: kind, kind master! He gives by the handful and never counts."

With these words he went straight into Melskyi's room. Ihnatiy did not dare to stop him.

Melskyi was still sitting at his desk as if petrified, with his eyes fixed on the white paper on the table before him. Not a drop of blood in his face; his tense breathing burst out of his chest, and on occasions only a very slight convulsive quiver ran through his

Detail of: *All Saints Church in Kyiv-Pechersk Lavra* by Taras Shevchenko.

body, and then thin colour would suddenly flash on his cheeks and as suddenly fade away.

"Is it you?" having turned around he asked Vasyl, who came in and stood facing him. "What do you say?"

Vasyl was only nodding his head slightly and did not say a word.

"Here, share this with your poor brethren and pray for... for me!" Melskyi murmured, grabbing his wallet and taking out a hundred-rouble banknote, which he gave to God's Fool.

"It is late!" Vasyl replied, as if holding his breath. "But, Vasyl will take. Vasyl will share with his brothers... Let it be!" Then after some silence he continued speaking at intervals: "Come what may! You cannot escape from it... Sooner or later... Does not matter... Come what may!"

Melskyi watched him bewildered − whether it was the solace expressed by God's Fool in his own peculiar way, or whether some other strange thought hovered in his impaired head, Melskyi could not guess.

"God be with you!" he said to God's Fool after some silence, gesturing to the door with his eyes.

"God be with you too!" Vasyl replied. "Yes, God be with you!" he repeated in an expressive and distressed voice that no longer exhibited the rudeness and lack of sound mind, with which God's Fool usually spoke. He turned around, walked towards the door, and, having raised his hands to the sky, he said only "Well!" − as if he had made up his mind about something.

His visit dispelled Melskyi's reflection. After God's Fool departure, he set about writing; then he rang, and Ihnatiy appeared with tearful eyes, answering the call of his master.

"What did you cry about?" Melskyi asked him.

"But, sir! What will... become of you?... of me?" And after these stammered words Ihnatiy began to sob again.

"You are a good fellow," Melskyi said. He stood up and put his hand on Ihnatiy's head. "Lead a proper and honest life... Here, take this for the time being," he added, handing him a bundle of banknotes. "And in here, neither you nor the others are forgotten. Pass this letter − if something happens − to my uncle," he pointed to a sealed letter that lay on the table.

Ihnatiy started crying and weeping even more, kissing his master's hands and swearing that his life would not be worth living if his kind master were to die. Melskyi was very moved.

Meanwhile, the hours flowed relentlessly, and the first rays of the sun had already beamed into Melskyi's bedroom. He raised the shutters and opened the window into the small garden of his apartment. The early birds were chirping in the garden; the morning was marvellous, and dew sparkled on the greenery. Melskyi stuck his head out of the window and fell into a reverie again. He thought that maybe this was the last morning of his life, and he would not see off the setting sun this evening and that night, the uninterrupted night, would stretch over him forever. Uncertainty of the future and the horrid step that he had to take – all that crowded in his mind and burdened his heart with a heavy load.

For a while Melskyi remained in this position. A light cuff on his shoulder brought him back from oblivion. He was startled and looked back. Before him stood Svydov, his second, and, at a little distance, both the witnesses for the duel who were officers of his regiment.

"Enough pondering about the vanity of this world," Svydov told him cheerfully. "It is half past five. We have one and a half hours left. Order them to bring us a drink and something to eat. You, my friend, don't become angry, but you will not get anything: fast for the time being. Such games are best played on an empty stomach."

In drastic cases, the calmness and good humour of a friend has a powerful effect on others, and that is what happened here. Three officers sat down cheerfully to the served breakfast. Melskyi sat down with them, even though he ate nothing. Svydov enlivened the conversation. He told his friends jokes and amusing stories about Melskyi; he declared that Melskyi deliberately made an effort to put on a forlorn face because he was going to the burial of his opponent, and so on. Laughter is infectious, and Melskyi had cheered up, especially by the end of the breakfast, when Svydov, followed by the other two officers, poured full glasses of wine, raised them and shouted aloud: "To your health, Melskyi!"

"I will thank you, gentlemen, in two hours and not before that," replied Melskyi in high spirits.

Svydov looked at his watch. "Oh, my friends, we were indulging for quite a while: it is half past six now. Melskyi, order them to bring your pistols and bullets: as executor of your life or death – do not go pale, my dear friend! – I want to examine whether all the ammunition is in proper working order."

The pistols had been inspected, the horses were summoned, and ten minutes later, the four friends were already riding through the countryside. With each step leading nearer to the place of the duel, the sound of horses' hooves on the ground rang louder and louder in Melskyi's ears. However, he himself was in good spirits – the natural or pretended cheerfulness of Svydov and other officers travelling with him had raised his own spirits. Approaching the designated site, they noticed the dust on the road and soon saw that behind them a few people rode, all at a trot. These were Melskyi's opponent and his assistants.

"We arrived before them," Svydov said, "and it gives us time to rest and smooth out the last wrinkles from Melskyi's face."

However, Melskyi was no longer the same: the determination, sense of honour and feeling of humiliation gave him extraordinary courage. His face beamed with absolute tranquillity; he walked freely and then coolly, but still politely bowed to his opponent's comrades, who arrived just at that moment.

Svydov and the artillery officer's second approached each other, exchanged a few words, selected and loaded their guns, and then, having split evenly the wind and the light between the opponents, momentarily measured eight paces to the barrier and then five more paces in both directions, for walking before taking a shot. Handing the pistol to Melskyi, Svydov looked at him intently, and was surprised and pleased with his calmness and composure, which were expressed in his features and in his manners. "Wonderful!" he said in a low voice. "For the first attempt at a duel it is too much." With these words, he made a few steps back and stood beside his opponent's second. The pistols had already been raised, the fingers were on the triggers, and the opponents had taken a step... the heavily charged waiting period took away the breath of the seconds and the witnesses... Who would be the one to fall? Or both? Both were equally courageous, both were equally firm... Only some impatience was noticeable in the artillery officer's gestures: it may be that this was a consequence of his usual temperament, or he, considering himself to be more offended, wanted to avenge the insult as soon as possible.

"Stop!" Suddenly a loud and firm voice boomed, and, with involuntary movements, both opponents lowered their pistols. Before they and their seconds could come to their senses, God's Fool was standing between the duellists.

"What are you doing?" he continued, in the same tone. "You are both wrong, but only you are to blame more," he added, turning to the artillery officer. "There is nothing for you to fight over."

"Get rid of this madman!" the artillery officer shouted.

"You are the one who is a madman because you bring innocent blood upon your head," said God's Fool, when the seconds and the witnesses on both sides seized him and wanted to drag him away. Vasyl was gifted with extraordinary strength – at least in this case, he showed remarkable effort – and six people could barely overpower him. Finally, after dragging him to the side of the barrier and seeing that he again was rushing towards his opponents, the officers, who were the duel witnesses, began to hold him, while the seconds took their positions again.

With equal fearlessness, the opponents again started walking towards each other: already they were almost at the barrier, already aiming; the hammer was lowering... A shot!.. "Stop! Oh!" And God's Fool fell, struck by the artillery officer's bullet. At the same moment, another bullet whistled above the artillery officer's ear.

Both opponents' pistols, as if on a cue, fell to the ground. Everyone rushed to God's Fool. He was still alive. A fountain of blood poured out from his flung-open clothes. The regimental doctor, who was invited beforehand by Melskyi's prudent friends and had been hiding in a neighbouring grove, ran to the sound of shots and, after examining the wound, he announced that it was fatal. Due to the close proximity, the bullet had gone straight through, and some of the victim's internal organs were damaged.

They began to dress his wound. Nothing serves as such a reliable step towards reconciliation between two opposing parties, as joint participation in one cause. Assisting the doctor in his actions, tearing their handkerchiefs and rushing as much as they could under the conditions to ease the sufferings of the poor wounded man, Melskyi and his opponent had not yet said a word. Finally, the latter, holding a compress on the patient's wound, while the doctor walked away to prepare a bandage, looked into the face of Melskyi, who was supporting the sufferer's head, and said with some effort, "Our duel is not over yet."

"Tell me, for God's sake, why have you challenged me?" Melskyi cried out spontaneously.

"You should know: was it not you who insulted me? Was it not you who laughed at my expense with the one whose hand I was seeking, and whose hurtful refusal I was not yet able to forget?"

"I swear on my honour that there was not a word about you mentioned in my conversation with Sofia. I would not have given this oath while facing your bullet. But now, over the body of this poor man, who fell victim to our affair, I must free you of these delusions."

"Why then, when she spoke with you, was she looking back at me and smirking sarcastically?"

"That surprised me as well, and I would like to find out from her the reason for that one day. But I repeat my vow once again: the subject of our jokes and laughter were others, and not you."

The artillery officer paused for a few minutes. He became thoughtful, and it seemed as if he was realising something. Then in a quiet and sorrowful voice he said, as if to himself: "This time as well, my quick temper and a suspicious disposition drove me to blank out my mind, to even commit murder. Oh, my God! But I have already been punished; without trepidation I must face the punishment that the law metes out to murderers."

Melskyi, feeling complicit, stretched out his hand and wanted to comfort him. The artillery officer grabbed his hand, squeezed it and said: "Will you forgive me my rashness and forget the offence I caused you?"

A young and kind-hearted Melskyi again squeezed his hand. He was quite satisfied: in front of his comrades, and consequently the whole regiment, he had proved that he was not afraid of gunpowder; he had made a sacrifice to the sense of honour, and his rival had asked him for forgiveness. What more could he demand?

Standing on his knees and without taking his hand from the compress, the artillery officer leaned towards Melskyi. They kissed.

"It took you long enough!" said God's Fool, who had just regained his consciousness. At this moment, the doctor came up and finished his dressing. The wounded did not make a sound but did not lose his consciousness again.

The officers came up to the reconciled opponents and congratulated them on their truce; Svydov, as a knowledgeable and experienced connoisseur in duelling affairs, was the first to say that both opponents performed excellently and that he would fight anyone who disparaged this duel.

76

At this moment, Melskyi looked at the face of God's Fool, who was calling him with his eyes. Melskyi leaned towards him. "I knew what the outcome would be," Vasyl said in a weak but audible voice. "God put it on my heart. I knew that I would lead you to your aunt's grave. Since your arrival here you have not yet been to her grave. Kind... kind was your aunt: she loved the impoverished brethren and gifted much to them. Vasyl was fed, clothed and warmed thanks to her! It has been ten years since she passed away to our Heavenly Father... That is why I liked you at first sight and wanted to get to know you better, but you had no time for me: the vanity of vanities captivated you. I wanted to thank your aunt for the bread and salt and said that I would prevent you from lying in the grave – and I prevented it."

God's Fool went silent. Shedding tears, a tribute to gratitude to humanity, Melskyi was not ashamed of them, realising that if God's Fool had not arrived in time, the bullet would have hit him directly, and perhaps also gone right through because the pistols, picked by the seconds, were big and generously charged – as according to philanthropic Svydov's reasoning, it would prevent the wounded from prolonged sufferings.

The officers went in different directions and, for a good fee, gathered together several peasants working close to the place. They were told to cut down brushwood from a nearby forest and make a stretcher to transport the wounded to the town. As soon as the good-hearted Ukrainians learnt that the wounded man was Vasyl, they did not even want to take a fee for his transport. They believed that the blessings of God would be upon them and their household for the service that they would perform for God's Fool. They were only astonished and whispered among themselves about how and by whom he had been shot. But Vasyl, having heard their words, said: "I myself, brothers, was asking for death. It was all God's will! Do not blame anyone here."

Listening to his words and believing them, for they knew that Vasyl never told lies, the peasants stopped their conversations. They put soft grass on the stretchers and a few coats over it, to make it even softer for the wounded. On top of that Svydov spread out his officer's greatcoat. The officers, as if in a funeral procession, followed the stretcher quietly.

On the outskirts of the town, the officers told the peasants to stop and knocked on the door of a small but neat house. There lived a good-hearted old lady, who was a widow. As soon as she learnt that it was about giving shelter to Vasyl, she immediately opened her door, prepared a small room and made a soft bed for the patient. The doctor readily volunteered to visit him, though he foresaw no hope of recovery.

Every day Melskyi came to see about his health, and every day he saw the gradual vanishing of the last sparks of life within this exceptional man. Vasyl spoke little and, when he did, he spoke about Melskyi's aunt, her virtues and philanthropy, sometimes adding short but strong guidance regarding the future of his life. All his words were lacking the signs of their former inanity and prophecy. Three days passed. On the fourth day, Melskyi, having found the mistress of the house in the entrance room, enquired after the patient.

"He is better today," the old lady answered. "He spent last night more restfully, and in the morning he spoke louder and more than in the previous days. He mentioned you. Now, it seems, he has fallen asleep; I went out for an hour and, after I returned, I did not hear any sound in his room – that is why I think that he is sleeping."

Melskyi slightly opened the door to the bedroom: there was no one either in the bed or in the room. The old woman cried out and ran to look for him around the house and in the small orchard. She asked the neighbours, but Vasyl was nowhere to be seen! Finally, Melskyi also went looking for him and asking around. One little girl told him that she saw how Vasyl, with great effort, had walked down the street towards the cemetery. Melskyi immediately went there. It was not too far to the cemetery from the old woman's house, and it could easily happen that Vasyl, during yet another fit of inanity, had decided to visit his last home. At the entrance to the cemetery Melskyi noticed a man sitting at a footing of a gravestone with his head resting on its low plinth.

Melskyi came up to him: it was, in fact, Vasyl, but his rigid limbs and blue face showed that life had flown away from its dilapidated shell. For a long time Melskyi stood thoughtfully over the cold corpse of the man who sacrificed his life for him. Then, examining the gravestone, he read that that monument hid beneath it the remains of his aunt. In his last days God's Fool had made a double tribute of his gratitude.

Detail of: *Vydubytskyi Monastery in Kyiv* by Taras Shevchenko.

"You kept your word!" Melskyi spoke. "You brought me to the grave of my aunt and came yourself to devote your last breath to the grateful remembrance of her. Rest in peace!"

In sadness Melskyi returned from the cemetery. Together with the artillery officer, who became the inadvertent cause of the death of God's Fool, they arranged a decent burial for this earthly sufferer and Melyski walked behind the coffin with his comrades. All who participated in the duel also paid their last respects to the departed. Crowds who had gathered for Vasyl's burial, even from nearby villages, showed in what respect this God's Fool was held by these simple but good people. The almsmen especially wept when they farewelled him into the grave – being a poor man himself, he had found a way to help them and share with them the alms that he received. A decrepit and skeleton-like withered old woman cried and howled most of all; when the funeral was over and when everyone left, she alone remained at the grave and sprinkled the fresh ground with her tears. After that she was often seen at the grave of God's Fool; whether she was his mother, or other relative, or whether she was an object of the departed's compassion – no one dared to ask her, and she never spoke of it.

GLOSSARY

Bandura-player (or *banduryst*) – Since the times of Kyivan (Kievan) Rus (9th–13th centuries) there were folk bards who performed religious and folk songs, as well as epic historical songs, also known as duma, accompanying themselves with musical instruments – the kobza, the bandura or the lira. The *bandura-players* were well respected and loved by the people in general. Often *bandura-players* were blind. Besides entertainment, the performances provided a source of education and news.

Bublyky (plural; *bublyk*, singular) – This traditional bread product is round in form and has a hole in the middle. Its texture is similar to that of a bagel.

Chorty (plural; *chort*, singular) – This mythological evil spirit is a male figure. A *chort* can change his appearance turning into a man, animal and so on. Often a *chort* is portrayed in the form of a man with little horns, fur, tail and hooves. Sometimes he has a snout. Like a human, a *chort* is born, gets married and has children. The *chort* is immortal. His main place of residence is hell, but on earth the *chorty* live in deserted places, at crossroads and so on. They have magic powers, which they use at night. Their main goal is to harm a person, to induce him to do something immoral.

Chumaky (plural; *chumak*, singular) – These 15th to 16th century Ukrainian traders imported mainly salt and fish from the coastal areas of the Black and Azov seas. *Chumaky* were admired and respected by the Ukrainian people for their bravery, as they faced the constant danger of attacks from Tatars and others during their travels.

Domovyky (plural; *domovyk*, singular) – This mythological male figure was often regarded as a type of house spirit. *Domovyky* share some similar characteristics with the house spirits of other European countries, such as the 'brownie' in England (sometimes called a 'dobby' in the north), but the *domovyky* have a very distinct nature that was developed through centuries of Ukrainian mythology. It was believed that the *domovyky* settled in the newly built houses of humans; however, rather than the people, the *domovyk* was actually the master of the house, and he was very much involved in the life of the family and household. When everything goes well, there is harmony and love among the family members, domestic animals are well looked after, and, in general, the household is in order – the *domovyk* is happy, he helps out and, when needed, warns the family of impending danger or misfortune. However, if the *domovyk* is not satisfied with how the home is run or if he is mistreated, even by accident, he can become vicious in his revenge – to the point of burning down the house.

Golden Baba – A deity of pre-Christian Kyivan Rus, according to Slavic mythology the Golden Baba is a goddess of peace, tranquillity and household welfare and the patroness of midwives.

Green Week – Also known as *Klechalnyi* or *Rusalnyi* (derived from *rusalka*), *Green Week* ('Zelenyi Tyzhden' in Ukrainian) falls before Pentecost. The name 'klechalnyi' is derived from 'klechannia', meaning 'green plants' or 'greenery'. During this week, among other rituals, the villagers decorate their houses with green twigs and wild flowers and herbs; one function of this is to protect the house from evil forces.

Horlytsia – This Ukrainian folk dance for male-female pairs sometimes includes an additional female dancer performing the leading part of *Horlytsia*, meaning Turtledove. The dance became famous in the 16th century and was also popular among kozaks. The accompanying music is rhythmic and is played in 2/4 time.

Hotsak – This Ukrainian folk dance is similar in nature to the world-famous *Hopak* dance with artistically performed high jumps.

Hryvni (plural; *hryvnia*, singular) – This is the unit of legal tender in Ukraine, with 1 hryvnia equal to 100 kopiyky (kopiyka, singular). The *hryvnia* has been known in Ukraine since the age of Kyivan Rus, and was the currency from about the 10th to the 14th century. The *hryvnia* was later replaced by the rubl, karbovanets and coupon until it returned as the Ukrainian national legal tender at the end of the 20th century.

Husli – This ancient plucked string musical instrument (also known as Gusle) dates back to the time of Kyivan Rus. Images of *husli* can be found on frescoes of the time, for example in Saint Sophia Cathedral in Kyiv.

Khorovod – In this type of ancient ceremonial circle dance the performers hold each other by their hands and move around a circle. The dance is performed while a chorus sings.

Kniaz (singular; *Kniazi*, plural) – This is the title given to the supreme ruler of Kyiv and its principalities during the 9th to 13th centuries in Kyivan Rus. The translations of this title into the English language, although not very precise, include Grand Prince or Grand Duke.

Knyshy (plural; *knysh*, singular) – This traditional bread product has folded edges, sometimes has a filling and is greased with oil.

Koliada – An ancient pre-Christian Slavic festival, Koliada falls on the night of 24 December and commemorates the birth of the sun.

Kozachok – This is a Ukrainian folk dance for male-female pairs. The name is diminutive form of 'kozak' and it is believed that the dance emerged in the sixteenth century among the kozaks. The dance tempo interchanges between rapid and dynamic movements and slow and lyrical movements. The accompanying music is rhythmic and is played in 2/4 time.

Kuntushy (plural; *kuntush*, singular) – This type of coat was worn by males and females among the Ukrainian and Polish population during the 16th–18th centuries.

Kupalo – According to Slavic mythology, Kupalo is the God of the summer solstice and the patron of marriage, love and procreation.

Lisovyky (plural; *lisovyk*, singular) – This mythological male figure is believed to be the master and protector of the forest, including the trees and other plants, animals and birds. *Lisovyk* is often portrayed as an old man, with a beard and horns, caring for a tree or a bird, or surrounded by animals. *Lisovyk* has no shadow. Each *lisovyk* has its own forest and lives in unreachable places. People may see him only when he wants to appear to them. Sometimes he is kind and can help people who become lost or will send animals towards hunters. However, at other times, especially if visitors to his forest have no respect for his domain, *lisovyk* can lead them deep into the forest, where they become untraceable.

Lysa Hora – Translated as 'Bald Mountain', Lysa Hora refers to a hill without vegetation where, according to Ukrainian folk beliefs, evil forces can be found, like witches who meet for their Sabbath. In Ukraine several places are known as Lysa Hora, and the most famous of them is near Kyiv.

Metelytsia – This Ukrainian folk dance, performed as the *Khorovod* form to a lively tempo, is accompanied by choral singing. Some features of the dance include fast interweaving of the arms and spinning that resembles a snow blizzard; hence the name of the dance *Metelytsia*, which is translated as 'snowstorm'. The dance is accompanied by lyrics that are sung by a humorous character.

Oseledets – An attribute of the traditional Ukrainian kozak hairstyle, the *oseledets* refers to a lock of hair on the top or the front of an otherwise closely shaven head.

Perevertni (plural; *pereverten*, singular) – According to Ukrainian folk beliefs, *perevertni* are sorceresses or warlocks with shape-shifting abilities (hence, the name, which means 'to turn'), who at will can turn into wild animals, birds, fish and insects or even into another person. *Perevertni* lead a double existence: living as either people or as animals.

Perun – In Slavic mythology, Perun is the God of war, thunder, storms and lightning. He is the chief deity in the pantheon of pre-Christian Kyivan Rus.

Pryzba – A low clay embankment, the *pryzba* runs along the exterior walls of an old-fashioned Ukrainian traditional house.

Rusalky (plural; *rusalka*, singular) – A mythological female figure, the *rusalka* is a kind of nymph. *Rusalky* share some similar characteristics with mermaids but have a very distinct nature that was developed through centuries of Ukrainian mythology. In Ukrainian mythology, the *rusalky* are the souls of young women, often brides, who have died an unnatural death, such as drowning or suicide. *Rusalky* are the daughters or wives of *vodianyk*, a mythological male figure who lives in water. *Rusalky* prefer to live in standing water – ponds or rivers that are still or have a slow-moving current. Usually, they come out from water in the warm months during the new moon. *Rusalky* are beautiful young women, with black or green knee-length hair (always loose) and bright black or green eyes. They are dressed in long, white thin shirts or are naked. *Rusalky* have no souls, but have hearts. *Rusalky* entice young men, luring them with their songs. They tickle them to death and take their bodies under the water. They also kill women if, after giving them a riddle, the woman does not give the correct answer.

Rushnyk (singular; *rushnyky*, plural) – These Ukrainian ritual cloths are embroidered or woven with symbolic designs. The *rushnyk* plays a significant role in numerous traditional and family occasions, such as weddings, christenings and so on.

Slastiony (plural; *slastion*, singular) – This traditional sweet pastry is often deep-fried in oil and dusted with sugar or covered with honey.

Sopilky (plural; *sopilka*, singular) – This Ukrainian folk musical instrument is similar to a flute.

Ternivka – A type of *horilka* (strong alcoholic beverage), the *ternivka* is infused with blackthorn.

Upyri (plural; *upyr*, singular) – These mythological 'undead' beings, most often male, are said to rise from the grave at night and attack people and animals in order to suck their blood. *Upyri* are the predecessors of Western vampires (Bram Stoker based his 1897 work *Dracula* on East European vampire legends and folklore); they share some similar characteristics but *upyri* have a very distinct nature that was developed through centuries of Ukrainian mythology. *Upyri* were once living people who suffered a sudden unnatural death, such as drowning or freezing to death, or those who committed suicide, or were cursed (damned) by their relatives. *Upyri* are friendly with witches and help them in their evil sorcery.

Veles – In Slavic mythology, Veles is the god of cattle, wealth and trade and one of the chief deities in the pantheon of pre-Christian Kyivan Rus.

Vodianyky (plural; *vodianyk*, singular) – These mythological male figures are water demons who rule the entire realm of water: wells, rivers, ponds, lakes, seas and oceans. In Ukrainian mythology, the *vodianyk* is depicted as an old man, covered in algae, who has a long beard and tail. According to some legends, the original *vodianyk* was once a man who drowned, while others reckon that he was one of the fallen angels. He can transform himself into various creatures: fish, animals and even children. If angered, the *vodianyk* can destroy mills and dams, cause flooding and drown people.

Yarchuk – According to Ukrainian beliefs, the *yarchuk* is a dog born with six claws that has the gift of identifying witches by smell and even biting them *(author's comment)*.

Zapikanka – A type of *horilka* (strong alcoholic beverage), *zapikanka* is infused with spices and is kept for some time in a hot oven.

Zhupan – A traditional, obsolete, most often male garment, the *zhupan* is a long coat. Since it was a rather expensive piece of clothing, it was worn mostly by Ukrainian nobles.

Zhuravel – A Ukrainian folk dance, the *Zhuravel*, which means 'a crane' bird, is performed to the accompaniment of the *Zhuravel* song. The accompanying music is played in 2/4 or 4/4 time.

Znakhar – A man known as a *znakhar* (or *znakharka* if a woman) is said to practise healing by using non-traditional means, including prophecy and sorcery.

ENDNOTES

1 **Ukraine** – In his works the author, referring to Ukraine and Ukrainians, uses 'Malorossiya' ['Little Russia'] and 'malorosy' ['Little Russians'], historical terms for Ukraine that were used in the Russian Empire. Modern usage avoids the terms as they are seen as patronising, implying a chauvinistic attitude towards Ukrainians.

2 **Bandura-player** – see Glossary.

3 **Podil** – This is a famous historic suburb in Kyiv.

4 **Knyshy**– see Glossary.

5 **Slastiony** – see Glossary.

6 **Yarchuk** – see Glossary

7 **Pryzba** – see Glossary.

8 **Belemnites** – These squid-like fossils are also known in Ukraine by their folk name, which means 'devil's fingers'.

9 **Lysa Hora** – see Glossary.

10 **Upyri** – see Glossary.

11 **Perevertni** – see Glossary.

12 **Lisovyky** – see Glossary.

13 **Vodianyky** – see Glossary.

14 **Domovyky** – see Glossary.

15 **Chorty** – see Glossary.

16 **Zhuravel** – see Glossary

17 **Hotsak** – see Glossary.

18 **Horlytsia** – see Glossary.

19 **Metelytsia** – see Glossary.

20 **Rusalky** – see Glossary.

21 **Sopilky** – see Glossary.

22 **Bublyky** – see Glossary.

23 **Kozachok** –see Glossary.

24 **Caves** – In this instance, the author refers to a 'cave monastery'. There are four well-known cave monasteries in Ukraine.

25 **Kytaivska Pustyn** – This is a monastery in Kytaiv, a suburb of Kyiv, which is located in the eastern part of the Holosiivskyi forest. It is now a national park, with a total area of more than 4500 hectares. The first recorded mention of the monastery goes back to 1716. Despite some interruption in service, such as during the Soviet era, the monastery remains active today.

26 **Pechersk** – The reference here is probably to Pechersk Lavra, also known as Kyiv Pechersk Lavra or the Kyivan Cave Monastery, which is an orthodox cave monastery founded in 1051. St Anthony and Theodosius of Pechersk, also known as Anthony and Theodosius of the Caves, were its founders.

27 **...bury them, even if secretly** – Those who committed suicide were not permitted to receive a proper Christian burial and be buried in the consecrated cemetery, according to the church in Ukraine.

28 **Borovyk** – in Ukrainian this means 'porcini mushroom'.

29 **Green Week** – see Glossary.

30 **Fern** – According to Ukrainian beliefs, fern is one of the most magical plants, which blooms only once a year, at midnight on Kupalo night. Its flower is protected by evil forces, but those who are lucky enough to find it will acquire magical powers: they will be able to find buried treasures and understand the language spoken by animals.

31 **To tickle** – According to Ukrainian legends, *rusalky* usually tickle people to death.

32 **Chumaky** – see Glossary.

33 **Kuntushy** – see Glossary.

34 **Romny** – A town in the Sumy region, during the 19th century Romny was known for its well-developed production of tobacco.

35 **Oseledets** – see Glossary.

36 **Zhupan** – see Glossary.

37 **Zaporizhia** – Here it refers to the Ukrainian kozaks' military and political organisation and their autonomous territory (approximately 80,000 sq km) in Southern Ukraine from the mid-16th century to 1775. Its centre was the Zaporozhian Sich, which consisted of several kozak strongholds on the Dnieper River.

38 **Zapikanka** – see Glossary.

39 **Ternivka** – see Glossary.

40 **To hand out rushnyky** – This expression refers to the ancient Ukrainian custom associated with asking a young woman for her hand in marriage. The suitor would send his representatives, called the *svaty* (*svat*, singular), to the desired woman's home to convey his marriage proposal. If the woman agreed to the proposal, she handed her *rushnyky* to the *svaty*. For further details, see Glossary.

41 **Bread and salt** – This is a symbol of Ukrainian hospitality. As part of Ukrainian culture, guests are treated with great respect. Even nowadays, the ceremonial custom of meeting a guest includes symbolically offering him bread and salt. 'Bread and salt' became an idiom meaning 'hospitality', for example 'thank you for your bread and salt'.

42 **Znakhar** – see Glossary.

43 **Kniaz** – see Glossary.

44 **Kassoges** – This tribe once inhabited the North Caucasus and was akin to the Circassians.

45 **Kniaz Volodymyr** – (958–1015) He was a supreme ruler of Kyivan Rus and is credited with Christianisation of the state. For definition of 'Kniaz', see Glossary.

46 **Perun** – see Glossary.

47 **Kupala** – see Glossary.

48 **Veles** – see Glossary.

49 **Golden Baba** – see Glossary.

50 **Husli** – see Glossary.

51 **Khorovod** – see Glossary.

52 **Kupalo Eve** – This night falls on the eve of 7th July. For definition of 'Kupalo', see Glossary.

53 **Nasoloda** – In Ukrainian her name means 'delight' or 'pleasure'.

54 **Koliada** – Koliada night is from 24 to 25 December. For definition of 'Koliada', see Glossary.

55 **Hryvni** – see Glossary.

56 **Duel to the death** – This is one form of duelling. Other forms include a duel until the first blood or until one of the participants is seriously injured. In the early 19th century, when the story was written, the duels were well regulated. Prior to the event, the seconds would discuss and agree on the type of duel and other requirements such as the distance, the order of the shooting, the walking allowance and so on.

Made in the USA
Coppell, TX
10 June 2024